BRAVE

DEEDS

Also by David Abrams

Fobbit

BRAVE DEEDS

A NOVEL

DAVID ABRAMS

AUTHOR OF **FOBBIT**

Black Cat
New York

A version of chapter 25 originally appeared in the
Provo Canyon Review, vol. 4, issue 3 (Summer 2016).

Excerpt from "We Real Cool" by Gwendolyn Brooks reprinted
by consent of Brooks Permissions.

Published simultaneously in Canada
Printed in the United States of America

First Grove Atlantic paperback edition: August 2017

FIRST EDITION

ISBN 978-0-8021-2686-3
eISBN 978-0-8021-8914-1

Library of Congress Cataloging-in-Publication data is available for this title.

Black Cat
an imprint of Grove Atlantic
154 West 14th Street
New York, NY 10011

Distributed by Publishers Group West

groveatlantic.com

17 18 19 20   10 9 8 7 6 5 4 3 2 1

for Jean

Lover, Cheerleader,
and the one person for whom I'd walk on blisters
all the way across Baghdad

"Tell brave deeds of war."

Then they recounted tales,—
"There were stern stands
And bitter runs for glory."

Ah, I think there were braver deeds.
    —Stephen Crane, *The Black Riders and Other Lines*

BRAVE
DEEDS

1

We

We walk, we walk, we walk.

We head into the fireball sun, packed in battle armor, baking from the inside out, throats coated with dust, hearts like parade drums, adrenaline spiking off the charts. We're alone, cut off from the rest of the brigade back at Taji, and now thanks to a busted drive shaft weakened in last week's IED blast along Route Irish, we are without a Humvee. We'll have to finish this on foot.

We double-time across Baghdad on our twelve feet, a mutant dozen-legged beetle dashing from rock to rock, confident in its shell but always careful of the soft belly beneath. We are six men moving single file along the alleys, the edges of roads, the maze of beige buildings. We keep moving: ducking and dodging and cursing and sprinting. We wonder how it could have gone so wrong so fast.

Going on foot was never part of the plan. That damn drive shaft—nobody saw it coming. And it's not like we can call for help—dial 911 or send up a flare—because we're not supposed to be out here. We're on our own and now we really have to keep up the pace if we're gonna make it.

The memorial service starts at 1500 hours. The last time we checked our watches, it was 1030. Half the morning gone. We may not make it.

From the back, Cheever calls out, "Hey, wait up."

"Keep moving, Cheeve," Arrow says, not turning his head as he jogs down the street. He's on point and he's focused. We wait for no one; we pause for no Cheeve.

"It's these blisters, man. They're killing me."

"Aw, somebody call the waaambulance," says Drew.

"My boots're filling with blood. I can feel it."

"Squish, squish, squish," Fish says.

"That's enough, guys," says O, his voice softer than ours: steel wrapped in velvet. That's O. He's never loud, but we always listen.

Everyone loves O. His full name is Olijandro, but we keep it at O—short, simple, sweet. Round as a bullet hole.

We have every right to give Cheever a hard time. He is, after all, the one who left the radio back in the Humvee— forgotten in our mad scramble to get out of what at the time looked like a singularly dangerous situation, an SDS. That's what Rafe would have called it, the kind of thing he was always warning us about—before he himself was the victim of the ultimate SDS.

Two hours ago. *Jesus, was it really only two hours? Feels like a whole week since then.* Two hours ago we were cruising along, taking the streets quick and easy. There was no laughter because we were on a sober mission, but we were feeling good. As good as we could, given the circumstances.

Park said he knew the way and we believed him. Why shouldn't we? Park is quiet, but smart. Not one to take risks. And today, of all days, we need to be risk free.

Everything was going fine. Smooth as a baby's shaved ass. Park at the wheel, Arrow riding shotgun, the rest of us crammed in the back: O sitting on Fish's lap, Cheever digging into his second bag of Doritos for the day, Drew sandwiched somewhere in the middle. Early morning locals in fluttering robes swished past the Humvee's small windows. Burnt shells of cars lined the curb, lingering memories of bombs. Billboards with soccer players saying things we couldn't understand, but offering us a Coke and a smile. Everything good and fine, then *bang*! It's like the Humvee decided it had had enough. *Sorry, guys. I'm calling it quits. You're on your own from here.*

You should've seen the look on Park's face when the steering wheel locked up.

This cannot be happening. Not here, not now.

Then came a hard *clunk*, and the Humvee shuddered to a stop. When we realized it wasn't coming back to life, we were out of there. Every which way in crazy panic, no time to stop and think. Even the Doritos got left behind.

By the time we regrouped two blocks away and Drew said maybe we should just turn ourselves in and call back to headquarters, we realized Cheever, our radio guy, was empty-handed and the situation had gone from bad to totally fucked.

A look came into Cheever's eyes and he released a string of curses.

Arrow closed his eyes, ground his molars, then said (over Cheever's *shit shit, damn damns*): "I know you're not gonna tell me you left the assault pack back there. Don't you *dare* let those words come out of your mouth."

"Just kill me now," Cheever moaned. He stared hard at the ground, his eyes boring a hole, digging the dimensions of a grave.

Some of us were all for doubling back and retrieving the PRC-119, but Fish shook his head and said, "Too late. Hajji's already scavenged the whole damn thing by now. We'd be lucky to find a single hubcap spinning in the gutter."

Humvees don't have hubcaps, but that's typical Fish—always exaggerating to make things worse than they were.

In this case, though, he had a point.

We blame Cheever. Never leave a PRC-119 in the hands of a guy like him. A platoon's radio operator is supposed to be the smartest guy on the team—like a Yale Law School grad slumming in the Army—but we ended up with someone who never quite mastered the call signs and treated the radios like crossword puzzles he couldn't finish.

Cheever is the self-appointed jokester in our little band of not-so-merry men. He'll go around saying things like: "Don't fire until you see the whites of their eggs" or "I'm so broke, I can't even pay attention." Once, when Private Cartwright slipped in the motor pool and came down hard on a trailer hitch between his legs, Cheever goes, "Ooh, right in the Balzac!" Lame-ass stuff that no matter what he thinks doesn't earn him any extra cool points.

Nobody's laughing at anything by this point. All kinds of scenarios unspool through our heads. We think about Jessica Lynch and all the wrong turns her convoy took in the labyrinth of streets. We remember hearing about a British journalist kidnapped last month. His beheading is now trending on YouTube. We think of those civilian contractors who were caught, strung up from the girders of a bridge, and then hung there for days after their bodies had been burned. They looked like big slabs of beef jerky swaying in the breeze. None of us wanted to end up like that.

So there we were, a cluster of dumb in the middle of Baghdad.

Oh well, at least we had a map.

We reached into our cargo pockets, unsnapped ammo pouches, probed fingers into pockets behind our flak vests.

Nothing.

We looked at each other, swallowing hard (none of us wanting to admit to the others that we were swallowing hard). We already saw how this would play out—like the surprise twist of a movie you can see coming fifteen minutes before the credits roll. If we were the virgin tiptoeing around the serial killer's lair, we'd be jeering and throwing popcorn at ourselves.

Arrow said we had to go back to the Humvee, take our chances, hajjis or no hajjis. We didn't argue. We needed the map.

Arrow led us back. We were half a block away—keeping to the shadows, hugging the buildings—and were about to turn down the street where the Humvee was hasty-parked with two tires up on the curb when Arrow held up a fist for us to stop.

We didn't need to be told. We'd seen the men and boys and some women streaming down the street, magnet-pulled toward something unseen. We knew what that invisible attraction was. We'd been such fools to leave the Humvee like we did.

We slammed ourselves flat against the wall of an electronics store. Arrow inched himself up to the corner, snapped a peek around the side, then pulled back just as fast. He looked at us, shook his head, then twirled his finger for us to reverse.

That's when we smelled the smoke and knew we were no-question-about-it fucked. Mapless in Baghdad.

We threw together a quick plan and made a good guess at our current location. Then we moved out away from the destroyed Humvee and the happy chants of Iraqis celebrating what to them looked like a victory.

Now here we are, slipping from building to building, street by street, trying not to call too much attention to ourselves in this city that already hates us.

"Arrow," Cheever calls again. He's still limping. "I'm not kidding."

Arrow doesn't stop, will not stop until we reach Forward Operating Base Saro safe and sound. That's the mission and he's intense and focused as a shaft whistling through the air until it thunks into the target at the FOB. Arrow's not his real name. He's tall and thin and moves like he's been shot from a bow. His real name is Arogapoulos—the letters squeezed together into tight, muddy stitchery on his Velcro name tag—but none of us could ever manage that, so we called him Arrow. It started after one of the company "fun runs" back at Fort Drum. The last half mile, First Sergeant usually let us break ranks and compete our way to the end. That day, Arogapoulos was leading the pack and he pushed hard all the way to the finish line. Slim, intent on purpose (*finish FIRST finish FIRST*), the breeze whistling in his ears. As we came out of the woods, Arogapoulos whipped past the entire company and collapsed to his knees, gagging on the grass in front of the barracks. Later, huffing from his own last kicking sprint, Sergeant Morgan looked at him and shook his head, grinning. "Jesus, you were like an arrow there at the end, Specialist A." So the name stuck. When Rafe christens you, you keep it.

"C'mon, Arrow—"

"Shut up, Cheever," Park snaps.

"Yeah, we're all walking on blisters," Drew says.

"Fine! Fuck all y'all," says Cheever. He lags behind.

Five minutes later, Arrow is forced to slow, then stop. While we pull security, Cheever unties his left boot. We surround him in a ring, M4 barrels pointed out, a bristling pincushion. We scan the rooftops, the windows, the doorways. Somebody could be up there right now with us in his sights, ready to take us out with one RPG. Later, we'll look back on this—at least some of us will—and think, *We weren't too smart, were we?* Bunching up in a cluster around Cheever, the fat pudge. But since we know Cheeve will pay more attention to himself than he will team security, we pull in close. Cheever has his good points, but selflessness is not one of them.

We are six men—Arrow, Park, Drew, O, Cheever, and Fish. And we are moving through the most dangerous sectors of Baghdad—the bubble of the boil—on foot now, thanks to the goddamn drive shaft and its microscopic cracks. We are on our way to FOB Saro to attend the memorial service for Sergeant Rafe Morgan and we are determined to make it there before sundown, alive, intact, all twelve arms and legs still attached. One team, one fight, one brotherhood. Just like the poster in our recruiter's office.

2

Foot

We're in a hurry, but if we have to stop and take care of one of our own, we will.

We look at Cheever's foot outside the boot. It's moist and raw—straight out of a butcher's glass case. And the *smell*. It's a sun-ripened leather bag full of vomit sprinkled with sugar. It makes our nostrils cry for mercy.

We all go, "Jesus, Cheever!"

"Moleskin," Arrow says.

Cheever drops his eyes, mumbles, "It's back at Taji."

Camp Taji, our home away from home, is thirty klicks behind us.

"Well, *that's* a good place for it," says Drew. "Better there than on your foot."

"Sure could use Doc right about now," Cheever says.

"Savarola, shit," Fish spits. "What a pussy."

"Hey," O says. "Doc's all right. He made his choice, just like we made a choice."

Savarola could have come with us, *said* he was gonna come
with us, but he backed out at the last minute. We waited around
the motor pool for fifteen minutes this morning—longer than
he deserved—until Arrow called it and said, "Looks like he
stood us up."

And so we went out into Baghdad on our own without a
medic.

"Wish he were here now," Cheever is still going on. "At
least he could give me some Tylenol to chew on."

"Suck it up, Cheeve."

"This whole day is turning out to be nothing but one big
suck hole," he grumbles.

There is a sound halfway down the block, a clang of metal.
A baseplate getting set into position, or the metallic mumblings
of crated artillery shells knocking together. We snap back into
the moment. Our M4 rifles come alert.

We wait. We listen. We watch.

Nothing.

"Stand down," Arrow says. "Jesus." He shakes his head.
"It's too early to be this jumpy."

We relax but don't lower our rifles.

Then O says, "He can have my moleskin."

"Bullshit!" we cry.

Arrow says, "You are not giving up your moleskin, O."

"Why not?"

"Because I said so."

They stare at each other for a long time—*too* long, if you
ask the rest of us. This is how it goes—testing a new leader's
boundaries, poking the bear to see if he'll wake and, if he does,

how hard he'll roar. They'll send over Sergeant Morgan's replacement soon—from Bravo Company or maybe HHC as a last resort—but for now Arrow is in charge of our squad. For today, a week—or, who knows, as long as a month if he's lucky. Besides, before he died, Rafe all but promised Arrow he'd get his stripes.

We're trying to get used to Arrow being the de facto squad leader. This day, this SDS we've gotten ourselves into, has called for one of us to step into Sergeant Morgan's vacuum. Given Arrow's time in grade—he got promoted to specialist long before the rest of us—it looks like he's the man of the hour. He doesn't have Rafe's stripes or his years—this was Sergeant Morgan's third deployment and he knew his shit—but on this day, things like that don't matter as much as they would if we were back on Taji.

We're all in the same boat. Like the rest of us, this is Arrow's first trip to the desert. We're all blind men feeling our way across Baghdad; Arrow just happens to be the one in front with the cane. Like it or not, we trail behind him.

O looks at Arrow, says, "It's just a piece of moleskin, dude."

Arrow looks away, scans his sector of fire, says nothing more. O does the same—after pulling a patch of moleskin out of his ammo pouch and tossing it to Cheever. We are silent, watching the street. After a minute, Cheever puts his socks back on his feet. As he laces his boots, he grumbles and curses, but that's to be expected. Cheever being Cheever.

We move on. Cheever limps but keeps up.

3

Sounds Like "Rake" or "Leaf"

We turn down a street with trees. A chest-high brick wall stair steps to a height above our heads as we continue down the sidewalk. Behind it, we hear something that sounds like a kid bouncing a large rubber ball against the brick. *Boing, boing, boing.*

Our skin itches. This heat is a bitch. The trees feel good and we slow our pace to cool our bodies in the shade.

Arrow looks back, sees how we're maintaining distance. We're textbook. Like ducklings waddling after their mother.

"Keep your eyes peeled," Arrow says.

"You said that already," Drew says.

"Well, I'm saying it again."

"We're doing all right back here."

"Just making sure."

Leaf shadows flicker across our helmets.

"Wish somebody would shut that kid the fuck up," Fish mutters. "He's driving me out of my skull."

O goes, "How do you know it's a kid?"

"In this heat? Who else would be out here bouncing a ball against a wall?"

"Someone who wants to drive you out of your skull."

"Hey!" Fish yells. "Stop bouncing that fucking ball, you miserable piece of shit!"

Boing, boing, boing.

"Some father you'll make," Drew says.

"Dude, I've got rug rats in every port. I'm doing all right."

"I'll bet you are."

The trees peter out. We leave the ball and the kid behind. We walk. Cheever limps, bites down on his lips.

Our gear clicks and clanks. Our breath is ragged with dust.

Arrow calls, "Hydrate." He's starting to sound like Sergeant Morgan.

We suck the straws on our Camelbaks without breaking stride.

We turn down another street, and then another. This one is narrower, hemmed in by a ragged assembly of buildings, awnings, corrugated tin roofs.

"Keep your eyes peeled, ladies."

We sigh. "We are, Arrow."

"Like an orange," goes Drew.

"Like a banana," goes Park.

"Like a halter top off my girlfriend's tits," goes Fish.

We have nothing to say to that. We've all seen Fish's girl and if she had saggy, heading-south-for-the-winter boobs stretched out by too many kids, that would be one thing. But she doesn't.

She's all firm and pert and high. Right now the very thought of her makes us throb with agony. Why did Fish have to bring her up?

Eighteen months is a long time. How will we ever get through to the other side of this tour?

Staff Sergeant Raphael Morgan was one of the best men we ever had. Rafe was what they call a born leader. He watched out for us, pushed us when we needed it, backed off when he knew it wasn't the right time to push. We don't want to put him on a pedestal or anything, but he really *was* everything we could have asked for in an NCO. He knew the field manuals inside and out, chapter and verse. He was prime time in the field. The sloppier, wetter, and colder the conditions the better. He encouraged us to find our inner warrior; he was relentless in his quest for our perfection; he made us hate him in the times we were exhausted, blister sore, and sleep robbed. But then that night, he'd sit down with us at chow, give us the lemon pound cake out of his plastic MRE pouch, and ask nothing in return (and not because he hated lemon pound cake—we knew it was his favorite). He was a used-car salesman when it came to persuading us to do the difficult, the near impossible.

He wasn't a big man, not one to loom over his subordinates with a barrel chest and a Sgt. Rock jaw, using his NCO stripes to bully us. He wasn't like the others—the bitter assholes, the career sergeants who delighted in our torment. Rafe never flaunted what he didn't earn. In fact, now that we think of it, he always seemed to be curled into himself, as if apologetic for his stripes and rocker. Like he was and forever would be one of us, a guy among guys.

He was short, a stump in the infantry forest, and used that height to his advantage, swimming below the sergeant major's radar when he was prowling for an NCO to blame for his own fuckups. Sergeant Morgan kept his head down—below shoulder level of his fellow platoon sergeants—and went about his work without unnecessary chatter and bluster. But the unwary were fools if they believed that quiet demeanor: Rafe was iron behind that black velvet. And man, he was smooth. We used to call him MC behind his back. Milk Chocolate. Goes down nice and easy.

We remember this one time back in the States, soon after we got a new commanding general. Word came down from on high that a weekend detail was needed for what turned out to be some special landscaping work around Fort Drum. Post beautification they called it.

Names were chosen, put on a roster, but they didn't tell us what it was all about until it was too late. Captain Bangor gathered us in a huddle after formation on Friday.

"Dandelions," he said. And we were all like: *What?*

"Men," he continued, "it seems the new CG's wife hates the color yellow and so we've been ordered to go out and pluck every single dandelion on post." And we were all like: *What the fuck?* But we didn't say that out loud, of course—not in front of Old Man Bang-Her.

It was up to Sergeant Morgan to get us through the weekend without all of us going to Officers Row, armed with knives, breaking into the commanding general's quarters, and stabbing him and his wife to death. Or maybe just dumping a bucket of yellow paint on their heads.

"Hey, guys," Rafe said that Saturday morning, our garbage bags fluttering in the wind. "This ain't so bad."

We looked at the parade field—the largest plot of grass on all of Fort Drum. It was a carpet of yellow.

"Sure looks bad," Arrow said.

"Naw, this ain't nothin'," said Rafe, giving us a milk chocolate smile. "Now 3-5, *they* got it bad. They been out in the field all week and it only stopped raining yesterday." (We knew this, but it was good to be reminded of Third Battalion's misery.) "You think they ain't sick of each other's smell by now? And they still got another three days to go. Sucks to be them. But here we are—warm, dry, doing a little gardening for the CG. Can't believe they pay us for stuff like this."

It was still a crap detail, and we bitched and moaned, but we moved forward in a line across the parade field anyway, feeling like we'd somehow one-upped 3-5.

"Besides," Rafe said as we bobbed and plucked, "ain't none of you heard of dandelion wine?"

None of us had.

"You never read that book by Ray Bradbury? About the kid?"

We stared at him, our faces not moving. Sergeant Morgan was well-read. We were not.

"Anyway," Rafe went on, "I figure we got enough to make at least a bottle apiece right here at the parade field alone. Just wait till we get over by the housing area."

We moved across the field, our boots sweeping softly through the tall grass and weeds.

"Golden flowers," Rafe said. "The dazzle and glitter of molten sun."

"Whatever, Sar'nt," we said, turning away to hide our smiles.

"Dandelion wine—like summer on the tongue," he assured us.

"Okay, Sar'nt." Our smiles gave way to laughter.

And so we made it through the day, picking dandelions and looking forward to drinking weed wine—which, as it turned out, we never made.

That was Rafe, always pulling us through the shit the Army shoveled our way.

That's why we took his death hard.

We were there that day, that most horrible day on our calendar of awful. We don't like to think of our Sergeant Morgan like that—the obscene pieces of him flying through the bomb-bloom air.

Yes, we took his death hard and, later, one of us might have gone outside to the solitude of a concrete bunker and cried until the snot ran, and one of us probably dashed for the latrine, vomit splashing the side of the toilet bowl, and one of us most definitely would press the tip of a revolver—a cold metal kiss good-bye—to his forehead eighteen months after our return. But we're not saying who. That's private stuff we won't share.

And so here we are, out in the bull's-eye center of Baghdad, on foot, moving through hostile neighborhoods with no commo and minimal ammo but with plenty of love for our dead dismembered platoon sergeant. Dismembered but not disremembered. We're doing this for Rafe and there's no turning back.

* * *

Rafe.

Not that we would have ever called him that to his face. Oh, *hell* no.

It was always, "Sergeant Morgan this" and "Sergeant Morgan that" and "How high, Sergeant?" on the way up.

But now that he's gone, we feel a closeness that erases rank so we'll damn well call him Rafe if we feel like it. There's no one to stop us from doing whatever we want out here on these oven-hot streets.

Rafe.

Sounds like "rake" or "leaf."

Something to do with falling, anyway.

4

Boots

Without slowing, Cheever looks back. No blood.
Not what he is expecting.

Cheever thinks he'll see a trail of bloody boot prints behind him.

Yes, his feet are still killing him. Yes, he's certain his boots are squishy with blood. And, yes, he *does* wish someone would call the waaambulance. But no, he will not keep complaining. He'll suck it up and drive on.

Cheever knows he's a whiny bitch and he hates himself for it. The world has never sat right with him. He's an only child and maybe that explains part of it, how his mother has always given him his way, from the baby carriage all the way through high school.

He didn't like the crusts on his PB&J sandwiches? Chop, they were gone. Hated the NPR station that droned when she drove him back and forth to school? Why sure, he could change the dial to 96.1 FM, the Rock. Pouted about the way coach always made them dress out for gym period? No problem—she would write a note to the school counselor and get him transferred out of that nasty-wasty class.

He at once loved and loathed his single parent who put the "mother" in "smother." He knew she did him no favors, raising him the way she did, but he wouldn't change a thing. Complaining gets him noticed. And that's what he wants: to be seen and heard and, above all, appreciated. Since arriving in Iraq, Cheever has had plenty of things to bitch and moan about (and trust us, at this point, we're fed up with Cheever and his mouth), but he wonders if maybe it's time to back off a little bit, dial it down a notch.

Right now, on this dismounted patrol across Baghdad, right here and now, Private John Hubert Cheever vows he'll keep his piehole shut for the rest of the day. Isn't silence the better part of valor? He's only dragging the squad down with his complaints and, let's be honest, he's the idiot who got us into this mess in the first place, isn't he?

Well, maybe not the *first* place, but it sure as shit didn't help when he left the PRC-119 in the abandoned Humvee. He's low man on the totem pole today and he knows it. That's why he vows to keep his lip zipped. That's what he vows somewhere around mile two.

Still, these blisters, man. Cheever figures he'll be showing up to Sergeant Morgan's funeral wobbling through the chapel door on two bloody stumps. Honestly, he can't feel a thing below his shins anymore.

Zip it, Cheeve. Zip it.

He deserves this. That's what he tells himself. *I'm a fuckup. A fuckup, fuckup, fuckup.* He steps to this cadence. *Left, right, fuck, up.*

I'm slowing them down. They'd be better off leaving me by the side of the road. Let the wolves come and eat me by sundown. Does Iraq have wolves? Well, it does now. Something bad and deadly out there anyway.

Cheever wants to die. Bring on the unhappily ever after. The end.

And he'd be glad to do it himself—one 5.56 mm round up through the chin—if only he'd get the chance, if only the rest of us weren't always hanging around.

Cheever wants to die a noble death in solitude. He came close one night a few weeks ago when he was on guard duty and Cartwright went on a chow run to the DFAC. When it was just Cheever, his rifle, and the moonlight, he'd come close to doing a barrel suck, fellating himself into the hereafter. A cloud moved across the face of the moon. It was a sign. Now or never. Hurry before Cartwright returns with the food and those pillow-soft slices of sponge cake tempt him to stay here in this life. Cheever had gone so far as to wrap his lips around the night-cold metal, but his hand stopped halfway to the trigger when he heard a soft cough—someone coming up the path behind the guardhouse. *Fuck!* He'd almost had it, for fuck's sake. But, like pissing and masturbating, this was one thing he didn't want to do in front of anyone else. He ripped the barrel out of his mouth—nearly chipping a tooth in the process—and acted like everything was cool when Sergeant Morgan walked up, doing his rounds as sergeant of the guard.

Well if that don't beat all. Cheever smiles to himself now as he limps down the street. Morgan is the one who kept me from killing myself, and now here we are, walking on blisters all the way across Baghdad to pay our respects to the body parts we scooped together into a dustpan and dumped into his coffin.

(Cheever, the idiot, doesn't realize there's no coffin at this service—only a shrine of boots, a down-turned M4, and a photo of Rafe. But we aren't gonna tell him that. Let him open his big fat mouth when we show up this afternoon and say something stupid like: *Where's the body?*)

Cheever has hated himself from the start. His father, a hard-drinking, chain-smoking college professor, died of a heart attack when Cheever was three years old. But he left his son the legacy of being named for his favorite writer (no relation, not even distantly). Ronald Cheever went so far as to name his son John Cheever Jr., though he was the first in the Cheever lineage to be named John. As a teenager, Cheeve had tried to read his namesake's work, but he couldn't get through even one story, scoffing at the ridiculousness of a man using pools to swim his way across a suburb.

But here we are, as stupid as that guy, walking across an angry city that hates us in order to attend a thirty-minute memorial service. Who came up with this plan anyway?

We did. We all did.

Idiots. We're all idiots, Cheever thinks as he grips his rifle and tries to keep up. His bloody feet slip from side to side in his boots.

The desire to die hasn't left him. He'll do this one last thing in honor of Sergeant Morgan, then when he gets back to Taji, he'll find a place where he can do the deed without the risk of anyone stopping him.

Who'll miss him when he's gone? Who'll care?

At the head of the line, Arrow stops, holds up a fist, and Cheever joins the rest of us as we sink to one knee. Cheever has been so wrapped up in the plans for his death, he hasn't been keeping his eyes peeled, doesn't know we've snapped to high alert. Now something is up and Cheever is watching the rest of us, trying to follow along, already half a beat behind.

Arrow motions with his arm and, startled, Cheever dives behind a parked car. He's relieved when Fish joins him.

"Thank Christ," Cheever breathes. "I don't know how much longer my feet could have held out. These fucking blisters, man."

See? He's already forgotten his vow of silence.

"Shut up, Cheever," Fish whispers. "Just shut the hell up. This is the real shit, you know. We could die out here today."

"Yeah." Cheever suppresses a smile. "I'm aware."

5

The Sprinter

There it is again. A noise, unnatural and sharp in the still air of the deserted neighborhood.

Arrow halts, holds up a fist, sinks to a knee. Like neighboring dominoes, we do the same.

Hsst! Listen. Watch.

Something is out there. A threat, an enemy, a crosshair moving over us, one by one. It's nothing we can see—not at first—it's just a feeling that comes over us. It could be the chatter-clatter of metal we heard a half mile behind us. It could be half a face peeping around a corner then whipping back out of sight when we dropped to our knees. It could be a bird flying in the wrong direction, a starburst of light from a second-story window, a prickle of unease washing over our skin, the fact that today is the thirteenth and it's thirteen minutes past eleven—any of those things. It doesn't matter what. We are all spooked at the same time and that is something we don't take lightly.

We're crouched, each with his own hasty hidey-hole: Arrow against the wall of a boarded-up café, O behind a lamppost, Fish and Cheever snuggled behind a Volvo, Drew pressed against a Dumpster, Park beside a palm tree whose upper half is gone, blasted away by American tanks in 2003.

Our heads are on the swivel. Behind our Wiley X's, our eyes dart north, south, east, west. Our breath slows until we are, without realizing it, inhaling and exhaling as one twelve-legged animal. In, out, in, out . . . in . . . out. . .

We are frozen for two minutes—tensed, watching, waiting for the threat to reveal itself.

The feeling passes and we're about to move on—Arrow even starts to rise from his knee—when it happens.

A man runs from one side of the street to the other—fast—like he's barreling down a track at the Olympics. Not something you normally see here in Baghdad. The locals are slow and deliberate, not sprinters.

Arrow gestures with his arm—*chop-chop!*—and two of us bring our rifles to our shoulders. We track the sprinter, our fingertips air-kissing the trigger, until he disappears through a doorway.

Our breath quickens.

Now what?

Five of us turn to Arrow. Mr. Large and In Charge.

For now, we'll follow Arrow—even when he does the most boneheaded, illegal act of stealing a Humvee from the motor pool and sneaking off the FOB under the noses of gate guards more interested in mashing thumbs across Game Boys than the loss of one three-ton government vehicle.

What we did this morning was absurd. We still can't believe we got away with it.

We all stole that vehicle and if there's shit to be meted out, we'll all let ourselves be splattered with muck. We did this for Sergeant Morgan, after all.

At least most of us did.

Okay, *some* of us. We'd like to think we're all in this together, but we'd be kidding ourselves. Like our opinions of the war itself, we are divided.

Some of us loved Staff Sergeant Morgan, some thought he was just okay, and some thought he was a total dick.

Likewise, some of us believe in this war, worship at the First Church of Bush, and have faith we'll find those weapons of mass destruction sooner or later. To them, Rafe's death was one of glory: he went out a hero, one more martyr fighting the good fight against evil.

Others think that's bullshit. To them, this is a job. Nothing more, nothing less. The starched suits at the Pentagon tell us to go *here*, we go here; they change their minds and tell us to go *there*, we go there. As long as we get a paycheck, we could give two shits about history and heroes.

But now we're truly out here, off the grid, on this illegal mission and the Pentagon wonks can go fuck themselves sideways. This is our game now—no rules. There's no telling what will happen before this day is through.

Arrow air chops with his arm again and, without question or protest, we rise and move, leapfrog fashion, overlapping in teams of two. Arrow says *go*, we go. We move off the street, out of the sniper's crosshairs, and make for the shadows, each of us slapping up against the wall of a building in succession. We surround the doorway where we last saw the runner disappear and wait for Arrow's signal.

He speaks the sign language of the infantry. He points at us, he points at the door, he counts down on his fingers: *three, two, one*. We nod, then melt inside to the dark unknown, rifles searching the way, heads on the swivel.

Drew hisses, "What the hell are we doing? Let's get out of here."

Nobody responds, like he'd never spoken.

Drew throws out one more: "This is stupid." But then he gives up and goes along with the rest of us as we begin our sweep and clear.

There's an Arabic shout, a door slams two stories above our heads, then the building goes quiet.

In the Land of Not Good, this is Pretty Fucking Bad, not at all what we bargained for when we stole the Humvee this morning.

6

Bad News

"Men, I'm sorry to be the bearer of bad news." Grimner's voice rang off the walls of what used to be Saddam's palace and was now the hive of our brigade's military operations. The LT's words struck the marble floors, spiraled upward, then echoed off the hallways, the dusty gilt furniture, and the wide white staircase. The words "bad news" hung in the air. "Last night, after doing all we could for him, we lost Sergeant Raphael Morgan. At 2200 hours, Sergeant Morgan expired from wounds suffered in an attack on his position while he was pulling security in the vicinity of New Baghdad."

Yeah, no shit, Captain Obvious. We were there, remember?

Lieutenant Grimner, as usual, didn't know what he was talking about. Rafe had died long before 2200 hours last night. He was gone the instant the bomb carved his body, eight hours earlier: brisket, flank, prime rib. That 2200 hours shit was just the Army's official medical time stamp. It took us that long to collect all the pieces and bring them back to Taji in a plastic tub.

Our lieutenant was young—almost as young as us, but that didn't mean we were friends, no matter how hard he tried (and he tried so hard he nearly herniated on a couple of occasions). He had no idea how much we hated the sight of his face with its rodent eyes and the curled lip, scarred from a childhood accident and frozen into a permanent sneer. Even when Grimner smiled, it looked like he was mocking us. His frat-boy bravado would get somebody killed someday. Back at Fort Drum, one of us had hung a dartboard on the inside of his wall locker with Grimner's official Army photo taped over the bull's-eye. After a week, his nose was nothing but a dart-speared hole.

Lieutenant Grimner coughed into his fist. "Sergeant Morgan was a—" He coughed again. Was he starting to cry? Was that it? Was our platoon leader crying? What a pussy. "He was one of the good guys. I don't have to tell you that. You saw it every day." Yes, he was crying; the corner of his left eye was twinkling. "And now the Army is going to honor his leadership with a memorial service. Thursday, 1500 hours, at the chapel on FOB Saro."

We rustled. Gathered in a loose formation around Grimner, we shifted from leg to leg, scratched our necks, stared at a spot floating two feet off the floor of the palace. Someone spat.

"That's the good news," Grimner said.

Good news? What was he talking about? Sergeant Morgan was dead—nothing good about that.

"The bad news," he continued, "is that, sadly, none of us will be able to attend. Well, uh, uh—I mean none of *you*. The commander and I will represent the company at FOB Saro day after tomorrow. The rest of the company, I'm sorry to say, is still pulling Quick Reaction Force duty. Third Herd is on mission to Basra—no way we can get them back in time. And most of First Platoon, as you know, is down in Qatar on R and R. That leaves us." Grimner coughed again, a bark to clear his throat. "This isn't coming from us, by the way. Blame Corps. In their infinite wisdom, they have seen fit to screw you guys over. The captain and I are sensitive to how you must feel . . ." He trailed off like a radio station going out of range.

Now someone said it out loud: "What the fuck? I mean, what the fucking *fuck*?"

Grimner held up his hands. "Don't shoot the messenger. I voted against the idea."

"Sure you did," someone muttered sotto voce.

"But Corps had more votes," Grimner continued. "Corps will always have more votes." He paused and his voice shifted to that just-trying-to-be-your-best-bud tone we hated. "Hey, I promise we'll make this up to you. Captain Bangor and I were talking and we're going to hold our own memorial service here in the company area as soon as we can. We'll honor Sergeant Morgan in our own way. You have my word."

Arrow shook his head. He looked at O, who looked at Drew and Park, who turned and looked at Fish, who glanced over at Savarola. Cheever looked at everyone else looking at each other and wanted in on whatever plot was brewing. Because, at that moment, an idea *was* percolating: dangerous, reckless, and born in the blistering heat of our mood. The hell with Corps. Who were they to tell us when we could and couldn't honor our dead? Did they not know who Rafe was? Fuck them and their fucking fucked-up rules. Bunch of headquarters-bound support soldiers—fat fobbits—sitting at air-conditioned desks in the Green Zone with Cheetos-dust fingerprints on their starched uniforms. They probably jacked off at their computers while they thought of new ways to screw us over. We bet we could go to the Green Zone right now and find a bunch of cum stains on the undersides of their desks. Well. Fuck. Them.

None of us spared any love for those fobbits and their bureaucracy. The Department of Departments. That was O's way of summing up everything wrong about the Army—like the Ministry of Silly Walks (O is a die-hard Monty Python fan), only worse because those fobbits controlled our lives, in their own cheese-dusted, fat-fingered way. Now they were screwing us out of paying our respects to the one guy we—most of us—truly loved.

Grimner was done talking and had dismissed us for the rest of the day, what little was left of it at that point. We went off to clean our weapons, eat chow, pleasure ourselves in shower stalls, take out our fury by killing Elites in our ongoing *Halo* tournament, read our books, write to our wives, and—for some of us—prep for Thursday.

We already had a plan. There, in the rolling boil of our anger at Corps, we six (seven, if you include that chickenshit Savarola) plotted our escape into Baghdad, our AWOL sneak-off into adventure.

And so, we cross Baghdad, passing through the chaotic center of terrorism—al-Qaeda, Mahdi, Ba'ath, and Badr clashing their ideologies and ambitions of evil—and we try to maintain composure. Straight-faced, even-keeled. That's how Sergeant Morgan would do it, given this FUBAR situation, this impetuous decision to risk court-martial (if not death on the streets before we can even get to trial). We stopped caring about our Army "careers"—whatever that means—four hours ago. It's us against the law. We're outside the law now. We're outlaws.

We'll admit this is foolhardy. It's just a memorial service and our AWOL adventure could lead to another six memorial services, but the ceremony isn't the point. It's beside the point. The point is—if we were to get this far in our shit-for-brains reasoning—the point is that we want to tell the command group to take their QRF roster and shove it up their air-conditioned fobbity asses. We'll show you! You can't keep us from honoring our beloved dead leader!

(Not that any of us would ever use a pussy-ass word like "beloved.")

We can't wait to see the expressions on their faces—Lieutenant Grimner, Captain Bangor, and all those colonels from Corps whose names we don't know. Bangor, what a joke. No one respects him. He's in love with himself, and that's the worst kind of commander to have. He says he loves us, cares about us, makes decisions in our best interest. But that's false-camaraderie rah-rah bullshit talk. He's too busy looking out for numero uno. Him and his always-with-him coffee go mug. When he drinks from the scratched and dented stainless-steel mug, air escapes from the pinhole in the lid and tweets like a songbird. When he raises the mug to his lips—which he does even when standing in front of us at morning formation—it sounds like he's trying to suck a terrified canary into his mouth. If we were betting men, we'd lay odds he'll bring that coffee mug to Sergeant Morgan's memorial.

We picture ourselves walking into the chapel on FOB Saro, maybe even in the middle of the service if we get there late, all of them turning in their seats at the sound of the door and the sudden splash of sunshine.

We'll be like a bride standing at the back of a church, all heads swiveling and all eyes focused on her as the organ stops playing, takes a breath through its pipes, then plunges loud into a fanfare. We'll sling our rifles to our shoulders, remove our helmets, and march down the aisle, smelling of dust, sweat, and broken blisters (Cheever). There will be gasps of surprise, of admiration, of anger. We will march forward, strong and proud at the end of this mission, our boots scraping the floor and our flashlights and compasses and carabineers clinking like we were walking Christmas trees.

Here we are. We did it. Y'all can go fuck yourselves six ways to Sunday.

Then we'll kneel at the front of the chapel, a six-man huddle around Sergeant Morgan's boots, his down-turned rifle, his photo. And some of us—okay, *all* of us—will let it all out. Not that we'd ever admit to a pussy-ass thing like crying.

From the front pew, Captain Bangor will sip-tweet his coffee, speechless and shocked.

7

What We Found

It's dark inside the three-story building so it's NVG time. The lightless stairwell calls for us to flick on the night-vision goggles, but we hate going green. When we walk through pea soup, reaction time slows and vision narrows to a tunnel. It's like being in a KROK 104.5 haunted house. Shit pops out in the jade dark and there you are, fumbling with the selector switch, the charging handle, the trigger.

That door slam is still echoing above our heads when Arrow chops his arm, sending Olijandro to the stairwell. Lead the way, O. We'll follow. We've got your six. We'll back you up.

One foot at a time. First one step, then the next, rising seven inches at a time. O's mouth clicks. His tongue has sponged out all the saliva. One foot, one step, half a foot higher into the unknown.

O thinks of that show he used to watch with his sister every Christmas: *Santa Claus Is Comin' to Town.* He remembers the tall, icy Winter Warlock who'd been living at the North Pole so long his legs were practically paralyzed beneath his white robe—ice freezing his veins, cramping his muscles. Then Kris Kringle started singing that song about how you put one foot in front of the other and in no time you found yourself walking across the floor. Even the penguins started dancing.

That's how O feels. He has to force each leg to lift seven inches to find the stair tread, then flex and pull the other leg up from behind and swing it another seven inches in ascent. O has to make himself believe he's the Winter Warlock breaking the ice from his calves.

He's point man. The job no one ever wants.

We get it. We totally get it. After all, we're doing the same thing right behind him. We're spread out in a line along the stone staircase, snaking up into the hot green dark of the building. We're walking, but toward what? Our breath is short and shallow.

Wait a minute, wait a minute! What the fuck are we doing? Drew was right. Are we obligated to investigate and pursue this runner? Couldn't we just shrug, pass him off as another nervous Local National, and continue on mission? We have a funeral to catch. Can't we blind-eye this one?

No. No, we can't. We're here to rid the world of terror. Find and destroy. Hell, *yeah!* If you see something, do something. This, after all, could be the scumbag hajji who hired the suicide bomber to drive himself into Sergeant Morgan and those kids.

Thinking this, our legs turn to coiled springs and we move with purpose up that stairwell.

O stops on the second-floor landing, holds up a hand, cups his ear, points to a closed door. He's heard something. We take our positions: O and Fish on one side, Park and Drew on the other, Arrow in the center kick spot, Cheever guarding our rear.

We listen and try to control our breath so it saws back and forth over our dry tongues with the softest of whispers.

Voices—one male, one female, one indeterminate—come from behind the door.

In that moment before we nod the go-ahead to Arrow, we imagine scenarios for what's on the other side.

One of us thinks we'll find dirty, dark-faced men and women gathered around a table holding screwdrivers and box cutters in their hands, tinkering with wires, timers, plastique.

Another pictures a firing squad of zealots with rifles, grenade launchers, and flamethrowers pointed at the door, waiting for us to show ourselves. There might even be a pissed-off female ninja, like in *Kill Bill*, hiding to one side with a sword, arms cocked and ready to chop off our heads as we move forward into the room.

At least one of us imagines they're making a porn movie and that we'll burst in on an orgy of jackhammering flesh.

As it turns out, it's none of those things.

Arrow leans back, raises his leg, and sends his boot crashing into the wood. The door flies open. We flow in, rifles raised. Cheever stays in the stairwell. He'll pull security while the rest of us do God's work.

A man, a woman, and a boy—faces lime green in our NVGs—cower in the center of the room, arms raised, empty palms turned to us.

We send them to their knees.

The man is our runner. He is still panting, but whether from fear or exertion, we can't tell.

We shout commands back and forth between ourselves.

"Left room!"

"Clear!"

"Stay down! Stay down!" we tell the man, woman, and child.

"Right room!"

"Watch our backs! Watch our backs!"

"Cheever's got it."

"There is no right room. This is it."

"The bathroom, then. Somebody check the fuckin' shitter."

"I'm on it."

"Cheever, how's it looking out there?"

"*Stay down,* I said. Down! Do you understand?"

"We're good out here, Arrow. Some lady down the hall poked her head out, but she popped back in real quick."

"Cuz we're Rambo Squad, that's why. You don't mess with Rambo Squad."

"There is no shitter."

"Whaddaya mean, there's no shitter?"

"I mean: There's. No. Shitter."

That's when we see a large stained bucket in a corner of the room. A couple of us lower our rifles. The rest keep them up and at the ready. It isn't certain which way this will go. We think of Staff Sergeant Morgan. What would he do if he were here?

The family stays where they are. Their arms must hurt at this point, but they keep them up like obedient little hajjis. The woman cries, soft as a prayer.

Park steps forward, makes them stand, then frisks them, moving the back of his hand discreetly, politely across the woman's body, just like we'd been taught. "We're good," he says.

Arrow tells them they can lower their arms. The man and boy do so. Then the man says something to the wife and she lowers hers, too.

We motion for them not to move and they stay where they are, frozen as if posing for a Sears family portrait.

We search the apartment for bomb-making materials, a weapons cache, Sunni leaflets—anything to explain why this dude (still panting and sweaty) would run away from us like he had something to hide. We find nothing. What a goddamn disappointment this door kick has turned out to be.

We taste the adrenaline in our mouths. It will go to waste. All for nothing and all because this asshole decided it would be a good idea to draw attention to himself in front of what Arrow has just dubbed Rambo Squad. We have to put all this nervous energy somewhere. Otherwise, this is the worst anticlimax in the history of anticlimaxes.

Fish steps up behind the woman and brings the butt of his rifle down on her head. There is a hollow *crack* like you'd hear at a baseball game. The woman gives a bleat that runs up a music scale—an *ohh!* exploding with breath—but it cuts off midcry as she crumples forward, knocking into her son on the way to the floor.

"There," Fish says. "Let that be a lesson."

"What the fuck, Fish!" three of us cry at the same time.

"What's going on?" Cheever calls from the stairwell. We can feel he wants to leave his post and come check out the action. That would not be advisable—not at this point.

The boy wails from where he lies beneath the woman's body, calling "Mama! Mama!" or whatever it is in Arabic.

The man shouts an unknown word and bends over the woman, lifting her, turning her. There is a dark comma of blood on her green forehead. Through our NVGs, the blood is black and though there isn't much of it, it scares us.

Fish has raised his rifle again—this time for the father— but Arrow stops him with a single word, a bark of anger and authority.

Fish relents, realizing he's about to get in even deeper shit, and backs off. We stare at him, not knowing what to say.

Fish. Shit. We should have known. Here's what Fish likes to do for fun: he'll grab an armload of Gatorade bottles from the dining facility and after he's emptied them, he'll piss in them all the way up to their necks, and screw the lids on tight. Then, when we're out on patrol with a crowd of thirsty kids fanning out behind the Humvee, Fish climbs up into the gunner's turret and tosses the bottles to them, calling, "Lemonade! Get your fresh hot lemonade, you little fuckers!" And then, slumping back inside the Humvee, he'll laugh and laugh and laugh.

"Hey, guys?" Cheever calls from the hallway. "I'm starting to get a crowd out here."

"Give us a minute," Arrow yells back.

"Less than a minute," Cheever answers, his voice winched higher in fear. A communal growl fills the stairwell. The neighbors are getting restless. "You want me to call for an evac?"

We say nothing. It'll come to him any second now, the stupid PRC-less prick.

"Oh, wait," Cheever says. "Never mind. No radio. Shitfire and damnation!"

Arrow kneels beside the family and feels around until he has the woman's wrist between his fingers. Now the man is sobbing along with the boy and he flinches when Arrow crouches beside him. He can't look at us. Arrow pinches the woman's wrist and counts to himself. Then he touches the husband on the shoulder and says, "I think she'll be all right, but you need to get her to a hospital right away. You understand? Mustashfa?"

Park, Fish, O, and Drew are surprised. We didn't know Arrow spoke hajji. Did our interpreter, that cool cat Hamid, school him during after-duty hours? It seems like something the eager-to-please Iraqi teenager would have done for Arrow.

Hamid. Shit. We could use him right now. But that's just wishful thinking. Unless we want him to translate through the knife slit in his throat.

Arrow says something else, a full sentence this time, ending with the upswing of a question mark.

The man nods. He still can't look at us.

Arrow rises to his feet. "We're done here."

We leave the room. Dark-green shadows line the stairwell, heads popping out of doorways, bodies standing with crossed arms thinking they can block our way, teeth flashing from behind lips. We gather Cheever and head back down the stairs, not looking to the right or to the left at all the people who have come out to watch. We push through the swarm of mutters like we're hot shit. Rambo Squad! You don't want to mess with us, no sir.

We spill into the street, panting and nearly shitting our pants from fear.

"Let's get out of here," Arrow says. And we do.

Cheever trails behind, saying on broken-record repeat: "Will somebody please tell me what's going on?"

*   *   *

We go three blocks before we stop and Arrow shoves Fish up against a wall, a forearm across his throat.

"Hey, hey, hey!" Fish gasps.

"I should kill you now." Arrow grinds the words between his teeth.

"Arrow," O says. "Easy, man."

"I should fucking kill you right here, right now."

A red Volvo passes along the street, honks its horn. It slows, takes a good look at us, then speeds away.

O steps in, pries them apart.

"What the fuck were you thinking?" Drew says.

We look at Fish.

"It was a moment," he says. "I just had a moment. Couldn't help myself."

"A 'moment'?" Arrow yells. Two sheiks in conversation down the street stop to turn and look at us. A curtain in an upper-floor window is pulled aside by the back of a hand. We're still not in safe territory. Nothing is "safe" until we reach FOB Saro. "Butt-stroking a chick is a *moment*?"

Fish goes, "Guess I lost it for a second. I got pissed off about the situation. Coming up empty—all that for nothing— the fact we were there in the first place, the tits-up Humvee, Sergeant Morgan, the whole nine yards. I just lost it."

"You lost it." Arrow takes a deep breath, then another. He's trying to practice Rafe's Three-C Theory of Leadership: calm, cool, collected. He's trying, but it's hard. How the hell did Sergeant Morgan do it, day in, day out?

"Okay," Arrow says. "I'll buy the rest of it, but not the part about Rafe. You could give two shits about Rafe."

Fish goes, "Hey—"

"Fuck you, Fish," Arrow says, putting his face too close to Fish's. "Rafe meant nothing to you."

"That's not—"

"Yeah, Fish," Drew says. "Fuck you and your bleeding heart. Why are you with us anyway?"

We circle Fish. No one says anything.

Arrow is still all up in his face.

"I'm sorry," Fish says.

Whoa. We never expected him to apologize. It totally takes the wind from our sails. Fish has never seemed like a guy who backs down. Maybe it was Arrow's arm on his throat or maybe, like the rest of us, Fish wants to keep moving, get out of this sector of the city. But whatever it is, he deflates us with an "I'm sorry" and we know we have to let it go. It will never be spoken of again, now that it looks like the woman will be all right. Will probably be all right.

Arrow spits again off to one side, the last of his anger balled into froth, and says, "Fine. Whatever. But do something like that again, old man, and I will butt-stroke you to death myself."

Fish smiles, slow and greasy. "You can try."

8

FNG

Fish is our FNG.

As the fucking new guy he stands at the outer ring of our circles, though he pushes against that barrier whenever he can. We know he wants to buddy up with two or three or maybe all of us, but we're wary. There is the designated FNG waiting period to be observed, after all.

Fish came to us three weeks ago from Third Battalion, where he was excess personnel, useless baggage on the roster, and they were always handing him shit jobs like head count at the dining facility and stirring the foul fires in the latrine burn barrels. He was glad to put that sorry-ass clusterfuck of a battalion in his rearview, and told us so whenever he could.

Fish is older than the rest of us. He might have even been older than Sergeant Morgan, but who knows. He has the worn-out look of a guy headed for the nursing home twenty years too early, someone who's been put through the Army's meat grinder once or twice. Between haircuts, there's a shine of gray at his temples.

This puts Fish at about fifteen years older than the average FNG.

The story on Fish is that he's been busted in rank so many times it's a wonder he's not pacing a cell in Leavenworth right now. Fish likes to brag he made it as high as staff sergeant once, two years ago, but then he was busted back down in rank—a quick plunge along the ladder—by a sergeant major who had it out for him.

"That bastard dogged me everywhere I went. He was all over me like stink on shit. Everywhere I went, he went—on PT runs, at lunch in the food court, even off duty when I went to go see a movie downtown in Watertown, there he was, sitting two rows behind me, watching me the whole time, never taking his eyes off the back of my head, until I couldn't stand it and turned around and said, 'Do you want to suck my cock, old man? Cuz it sure seems like you're in love with me.' I guess he didn't take too kindly to that. Or to the punch I threw when I cornered him in the parking lot afterwards. That guy was a slimeball and deserved everything I gave him."

That's how we heard it from Fish. We doubted it was the whole story.

So, here he is—the old man of the squad, but the lowest ranking. You can see how well he's been taking this. Just ask that lady in the apartment we're running from.

We've only known Fish three weeks, but most of us already hate him. He replaced Cunningham, a nice guy we all loved until he was killed in an IED blast a month before the one that got Sergeant Morgan.

Fish never got to know Rafe like we did, so we're not sure why he's so gung-ho to be out here on this covert memorial mission. We figure he just wants to get off the FOB for a day. Or maybe he's looking for adventure—a story he can tell chicks in bars once we get back.

That seems more like Fish's style, the fucking new guy.

9

Grand Theft Humvee

We never expected to get this far.

Four hours gone and here we are, still strolling around Baghdad like tourists. By this time, someone back at Taji has put out an APB for us—a be on the lookout for a cluster of dumb fucks wandering lost and alone. Why we haven't already been scooped up by another unit or a roving patrol of Iraqi police is a mystery to us.

We figure we'll get caught soon. It's only a matter of time before the Humvees pull up in a swirl of dust and barked commands.

We won't go easy.

We don't care if we're BOLO'ed. Do you know who we are? We're running the Sergeant Morgan Memorial 10k and you are seriously fucking up our finish time. Out of our way!

That's what we'll scream, all the way down to the ground, fighting the zipties on our wrists.

But that's later. For now, we need to continue our mission. Put some pep in our step, as Sergeant Morgan used to say.

We walk on, hustling away from the skull-cracked woman.

We're in a race now. It had started out a sure thing this morning. And then it all went to shit.

We think about that lottery-winning moment when it looked like we were getting away with this. We raided the motor pool before dawn when it was empty, the mechanics grabbing an early breakfast. We'd planned a predawn start, giving ourselves a cushion of several hours. Good thing, because now it looked like we'd need every ounce of stuffing in that cushion. If we got to FOB Saro early, Arrow said, we could just fuck around for a few hours: go see a movie, stop by Burger King for some Whoppers, cruise the streets in search of hot chicks. Ha!

"It's what Rafe would've done if he were in our shoes," Arrow said. There was a hitch and catch in his voice the rest of us pretended not to notice.

Out of all of us, Arrow seems to be taking Rafe's death the hardest.

We think Sergeant Morgan would have approved of the plan, especially how Arrow drew a sand table for us last night and then, when he was certain we understood, swept it away with the side of his boot. We all fist-bumped in agreement (even Park, who was usually allergic to these things), then went back to our hooches to catch whatever sleep we could before the agreed-upon hour our watches would beep us awake.

But none of it seemed real until the moment we snipped the lock with bolt cutters, unchained the steering wheel, and brought the Humvee to life with a purr. Then Park rolled out across the FOB—*slow, slow, slow*—tires crunching gravel. Arrow rode shotgun, the rest of us hunkered down in the backseat. The

FOB's streets were emptied of all but a few ambitious joggers, their yellow-green safety belts worn like beauty-queen sashes across their chests, reflecting a jagged slash from our headlights. We rolled slow, slow, slow past Burger King, the bowling alley, the chapel, the headquarters building. Soldiers reporting for morning shift passed through the front door checkpoint, flashing their badges and pausing in the smoke shack to take a few deep, hasty drags from their cigarettes before they had to go sit on their asses at a desk for the rest of the day. We grinned at how we were gonna royally fuck up someone's day at headquarters, all that paperwork needing to be filed for this joyride of ours. We laughed as we rolled through Taji's streets, a slow-motion escape from authority.

Then we were at the Entry Control Point, the funnel-choke of security for the forward operating base. We sucked in a breath and held it.

Arrow convinced them. He got out of the passenger door, went inside the guard shack with a handful of papers—discarded op orders we'd pulled out of Captain Bangor's trash can last night when no one was looking. Arrow held a thumb over the date in the upper right corner of the paper he showed the guards and somehow convinced them we were legit. He looked at that pair of fobbits—a couple of lazy asses we'd probably roused from a nap, busted while dreaming of marshmallow clouds and cupcake kingdoms—and said something to them that loosely translated to: "These aren't the droids you're looking for."

And, get this, they'd nodded like hypnotized storm troopers and waved us on. The next thing we knew, we were winding through the concrete barriers—amazingly, incredibly, ridiculously free of the FOB.

We slipped away from Taji like fish finding a hole in the net.

"Woo!" said Drew.

"Hoo!" answered Cheever.

We cheered as we sped out onto the highway that would take us to the memorial service.

Grand theft Hummer. We were living the thug life now. We were unstoppable.

10

We Real Cool

"We real cool!"

Our huff-pant voices called back: "We real cool!"

"We left school!"

"We left school!" Our hundred feet soft-clumped in unison on the paved road snaking through Taji. Sergeant Morgan kept pace at our left and called cadence, barking into the dusty morning air. This was two months before his death—about halfway through this deployment—and he was pushing us hard. As always.

"We lurk late!"

"We lurk late!"

This was one of Rafe's favorite cadences—a home-brewed chant he started back when we were at Fort Drum. He said it was one of his favorite poems, broken down into pieces so we could—*real cool*—get some book schooling with our morning PT.

"We shoot straight!"

He told us the poet's name once, but none of us can remember it now. And that makes us sad. We know Rafe would want us to remember this poet even more than he'd want us to remember him. Shit like that was always important to him. He wanted us to be smarter than we thought we could be.

"We shoot straight!"

And these are the kind of things we liked to remember about him: the way he hardly broke a sweat on the five-mile runs every Friday through Taji; the way his teeth gleamed as he called cadence, quick bursts of ivory across his dark face; the way he pushed us through that last mile even though the heat of the day had already started to drain us; the way he sang the word "cool" like it was a glass of ice water waiting for us at the finish; the way he was always out there to our left, encouraging us, goading us, moving up and back along the formation with his teeth and voice; the way it felt like he'd always be there; the way it seemed he'd never leave us.

"We jazz June!"

We didn't know what the fuck that meant—*Rafe and his fancy poets*—but we sang it anyway: "We jazz June!"

We dug deep. We pushed hard to the finish line.

"We die soon!"

11

Solitude

We craved it; none of us got it. We could never find a hidey-hole of *alone*. Peace and quiet and time just to be in our own fucking mind? Hard as catching windblown sand.

The war was always with us. It tattooed our skin, it clothed us in sweat and sand and blood. It was bright as the eyeball-searing lights set up at nighttime checkpoints, rolled in on generators, poles extended twenty feet into the air, dazzling like the alien landing pad at the base of Devils Tower in *Close Encounters of the Third Kind*, a movie we all remember seeing as kids. The scientists and government spooks and that weird French guy all had to wear sunglasses at night to keep from being blinded by the mother ship. That's our war: a mother ship descending with subsonic, glass-shattering hums. Lights blinking everywhere. We wear sunglasses at night.

We cannot escape the war. The distant fireworks squeal of mortars falling two miles away, the soft *thud* of impact, the rattle of gunfire like boots walking across Bubble Wrap, the slow cough of Humvee engines coming to life. War is our soundtrack.

We cannot get away from our "warself." Not in the dining facility, or the narrow gravel lanes between our hooches, or the squeeze inside a Humvee. Not in our cots at night, not in the morning shower stall. Not even in the rancid "solitude" of the porta-potty where we are hemmed in by walls of graffiti, the overlapping chatter of profanity:

Cpl. Jennifer Swardos is the mayor of Twatsville (Population: Everybody)

If you ain't Muslim, you ain't Shiite

If you ain't feces, you ain't shit

We Flawda Boyz bout to lay all these iraqis to bed. Holla out. —Your Boi

Coles was here Sept. 2004 to April 2005.

Beneath that, someone else wrote:

That's a long time to take a shit!

We can close our eyes, clap our hands over our ears, but the war remains in our head. It's a sound that never stops.

12

Arrow

We'll admit we're men of flaws. What infantry company, corporate office, university teaching staff or night-shift crew at McDonald's *isn't* made up of imperfect people?

Looking at us marching across Baghdad, risking death to attend a funeral, you might think we're great men on a brave mission: poster-worthy heroes with brass balls and solid-gold hearts.

But you'd be wrong. We are fucked up and flawed.

Take Arrow, for instance. He doesn't get along with his parents. In fact, he hates them.

It's not like they beat him as a child, or were alcoholics, or loved his sisters more than him. But there was a determined indifference tainting the Arogapoulos household all the years of his childhood. Arrow was a swimmer at sea, bobbing in the waves, semaphoring his arms, yelling for his parents' attention as they sailed past on the yacht of their marriage, pretending not to see or hear him as they stood there on deck, their backs pressed against the railing, deep in conversation with the only person who mattered in their lives: each other. Arrow's father, a vice president at the savings and loan, and Arrow's mother, a ballerina who'd lost her bloom early and now ran a yoga studio, had enough patience and concentration for just one other person. They poured all their focus into the partner who shared the marital bed, leaving all others outside their sphere—including, and especially, their three children. Many were the nights Farris and Linda Arogapoulos went bowling, took in a movie, or set out on meandering drives that took them to neighboring towns to attend wine tastings, jazz festivals, and once an AKC dog show, leaving their three children behind, barely remembered during their carefree middle-age dates.

Linda used to joke, looking directly at her son Dmitri: "You're nothing but a forgotten trip to the drugstore, my dear."

"Or a hole in the rubber," Farris cracked, holding up his half of the vaudeville show. Not that they didn't keep up appearances as good parents—God knows, Mill Valley was too small for them to be anything but bright, shining examples of encouragement and support in the superficial areas at which all parents excel: chauffeuring to ballet class and piano lessons, pumping fists at the Cub Scout pinewood derby victories, engaging teachers with smart, pointed questions at school conferences. That was the mask. They gave off airs of being liberal parents who gave a shit. But when the front door was closed and the drapes were drawn—*snap!*—their smiles would twinkle out and they'd go off to separate rooms to pursue with laser-focused selfishness their hobbies and patterns: checking e-mail (so new and exciting in the late nineties), reading brick-size novels about English country estates, polishing the coin collection, cooking, drinking, and bowling, oh so many nights of bowling.

Dmitri, Brenda, and Lindsey came of age under the care of a succession of babysitters, teenage proxies for their real parents, girls (always girls, Farris and Linda never trusting a hormonal male alone with their daughters) who made popcorn, allowed them to watch forbidden TV, didn't care if they brushed their teeth or not, got down on the floor with them to play Candy Land, or—the worst ones—sat sullen and distracted on the sofa with a book, shushing the three brats every five minutes with a "God, shut *up*, will you? Can't you see I'm trying to read?"

And so, Dmitri, Bren, and Lindy-loo grew up without compasses. Arrow didn't know how his sisters felt, but for *his* part, he longed for guidance, a goddamn rudder in the ocean, someone to take him by the shoulders, point him in a direction, and say, "Go this way for x number of miles, then turn south when you get to x location in your life, and hang a right two years later." Arrow hated drifting. All through grade school, on into junior high and, especially, high school, he floundered, beating his arms against the sea current, growing more and more afraid of what lay in wait for him outside the Arogapoulos house, but at the same time longing for the day when he could escape Mill Valley. He often thought of slipping out in the middle of the night—when Farris and Linda were late returning from the Sonoma wine and cheese festival, for instance—and running to the bus station. But that frightened him more than staying. Where would he go? How would he eat?

He got his answer on Career Day during his senior year when a stocky, buzz-cut sergeant pulled him aside and lured him into his booth. Inside there was a gallery of photos velcroed to the blue fabric walls displaying images of beaming men and women in clean uniforms and skin toasted by a life spent outdoors in the woods, deserts, and oceans—people who looked like they had direction, purpose, compasses. Arrow listened, liked what he heard, and signed the papers that very afternoon. When he announced this to Farris and Linda—who were home for a rare dinner with their children that night—he was greeted with: "Well, if that's really what you want to do . . ." Their indifference was all the answer he needed. And so, Arrow entered the Army, grateful for its structure and discipline. As the years went by and he talked to fellow soldiers and gained some perspective, he realized his parents had royally screwed him over, robbing him of a life most American teenagers seemed to have enjoyed.

In fact, Rafe was the one who made Arrow take a rearview look at his family life.

During his quarterly counseling sessions, Sergeant Morgan would always hurry through the official checklist of what the Army required him to talk about, and then he'd get right down to the part he liked the best: having a personal conversation with his soldiers, not only about their duty performance, but about what made a good soldier, a good citizen. Rafe liked to use himself as an example.

"Now take me, for instance," he told Arrow one time when they were sitting across the desk from each other at Fort Drum. "Contrary to what you might think by looking at the color of my skin, I was not raised by a single mother on welfare, I was not a crack baby, I didn't grow up in the projects—"

"I didn't think anything like that, Sergeant," Arrow said quickly—even though, if he was honest, that's kind of what he *had* assumed.

"I was born and raised in Indianapolis in a happy, healthy, stable home," Rafe said, steamrolling over Arrow's protest.

"Father a schoolteacher, mother a lawyer. They gave me everything a kid could want: love, attention, three square meals a day, help with my homework, a library card, birthday parties at Chuck E. Cheese, the whole nine yards. But you know what, Specialist A.?"

"What, Sergeant?"

"It wasn't enough. No sir, it wasn't enough. I always felt like there was something lacking, some—some—" He searched the air for a word with his fingers until he found it. "Some *purpose* in life."

To this day, Arrow isn't sure if he gasped out loud or just in his head.

Rafe continued to talk, as if Arrow hadn't made a sound: "They were the best parents in the world, but they couldn't tell me what to do with the rest of my life. That's one thing I had to discover on my own. And boy did I find it." He grinned. "I guess you know the answer to *that* million-dollar question, huh?"

"The Army," Arrow said.

"That's right, the Army. I tell you what, I never knew who I was until I put on the uniform."

Arrow can't remember what they'd been talking about at the time: the military code of conduct? Improving his score at the rifle range? His need to loosen up and be more friendly with the others in the platoon? Or maybe this was one of those times Rafe went off on a tangent and Arrow just nodded along. Whatever the case, his NCO's words had stuck.

"I think I know how you feel, Sergeant," Arrow said. "And I appreciate you telling me all that, I really do."

"That's what I'm here for, Arrow. That's my goddamn mission in life: looking out for the good ones like you."

(Arrow didn't know it at the time, but that's the moment when his feelings for Rafe changed. If you'd asked him about it, his head would have balked and scoffed. But his heart knew otherwise.)

Sergeant Morgan had him sign the counseling form, then as he stapled the papers together he gave Arrow a deep look and said, "I can tell you didn't always have it easy growing up, Dmitri."

Arrow must have had a shocked expression on his face because Rafe smiled and said, "Don't ask me how I know—I just do. But the point I was going to make is, that doesn't matter. You left that family behind when you raised your right hand and swore the oath. You don't belong to them anymore. You belong to us. And I hope you see that as a good thing."

Arrow's throat had gone dry, but he managed to whisper: "Yes, Sergeant. Yes, I think I do."

He left Rafe's office that day feeling loose and light. His blood beat hard and fast.

Arrow often wondered what he would have been like if his parents had actually ever given a shit about him adrift on those waves, if Farris and Linda had ever once looked over the deck railing and thrown him a life preserver—just once. He grew to hate his parents and, though this saddened him to a degree, he stopped calling them after that counseling session with Rafe, stopped e-mailing, and all but wrote them out of his life. They didn't even know he was here in Iraq. He could die on this Baghdad street—a blood spurt at the end of a bullet's trajectory—and they wouldn't know until the casualty assistance officers showed up on their doorstep. Provided they weren't at bowling league that evening.

13

O

O's flaw? He loves his ex-wife too much.

And that distraction could get him killed today.

We worry about O. He's too soft and daydreamy. Which makes him the perfect candidate to be a bullet sponge. We know he can't help it. We know O thinks of her all the time. We don't blame him. Not that O's ex–old lady is hot or even lukewarm—her looks are stretched and softened by too many kids—but like O, she's kind and gentle and that makes her hot in her own MILF-y way. We can see why she's always in O's head.

We're on something like mile three of our Sergeant Morgan memorial hike and the heat and the pavement and the dust are killing us. But not O. His head is all rainbows and kittens and heart-shaped candy boxes.

And the e-mail he sent his ex-wife last week. Still unanswered.

Melinda, mi corazón. My dear, sweet Melinda. How are you, my darling? Did you get the letter I mailed two weeks ago? It should have gotten to you by now. Do you like the stationery? I picked it out at the PX with you in mind. It's a nice color, I thought. Maybe not your

59

favorite, at least not that I remember. By now, maybe you've changed colors and I don't know what the new one is. People change. I know this, ya lo sé. There's so much I don't know about you since—you know, since the split. You've moved on to new colors, new foods, a new town, maybe new lovers. Por Dios, it hurts to think that. It hurts too much, so I'll keep pretending it's not true, that you haven't taken anyone else into your bed, that you've kept it sacred as our bed—at least in your heart. Have you kept it sacred? Is it still our bed? Let's make it our bed again when I get back, Melinda. Let's try. That's what I said in the letter, in case you haven't read it yet. I said let's try again when I get back. Let's give it another go. If you're willing, I think we can work it out. If there's one thing I've learned over here, it's that we never have enough time to get everything right. So what if you and I had problems? Everyone, todo el mundo, has problems and we just have to work through them. Life is too short to worry about getting everything perfect. You're going along, working hard, and then BAM your life gets chopped off—the end, se acabó—I've seen this happen over here nearly every day. CHOP-CHOP you're through and you never managed to make things right with the ones you've hurt. I've given this a lot of thought. I want to make it right with you, Melinda. It doesn't have to be like the way it was before. It won't be like that. I see things better now. I understand how it needs to be, how I need to be. I think I've changed. I hope I've changed enough for you, mi amor. I think we can put us back together, only better this time. I'm willing to—

Okay, that's enough. We can only take so much of this hearts-and-flowers shit. But you get the idea. O needs to keep some situational awareness out here today if he ever wants to get back to Melinda, his corazón.

14

James and Jinx

The sprinter and his son will be fine. The mother will live. Fish is okay. Everything's good. We real cool.

Keep walking. Put one foot in front of the other and soon you'll be walking across the floor. That's Baghdad Survival 101.

We can do this, despite the setbacks. What mission doesn't have setbacks and roadblocks, right? We've been through worse.

That time in Baqubah, for instance. The one with the dogs. That was a bad one.

The first dog was black with a patch of white at his throat in the shape of a bow tie. That's why Sergeant Morgan named him James Bond—that, and the fact he was cool as a martini, total stealth, slipping in and out of the company area on Taji like a shadow flickering at the periphery of our sight.

We all loved the dog: from the time Sergeant Morgan showed up with him one night, saying, "Hey, look what I found," to that last blood-spattered moment inside the armored personnel carrier. JB was a good mutt. Like Rafe, he didn't deserve what he got.

The dog was illegal. He broke every regulation the generals and sergeants major decreed once we were over here in the sandbox (dreamed up out of late-night bullshit sessions in those first days of the war when they sat around a table lit by kerosene lanterns and said to themselves: "Gentlemen, how can we legally make our soldiers' lives harder and more unbearable?"). But we could give two shits. We found James Bond—or *he* found *us*—and it was finders keepers all the way to the end.

Sergeant Morgan later told us he'd been checking on Gerard and Buckley, who were pulling guard shift that night. "The dog came out of nowhere, thought he was gonna attack me, until I remembered I'd smuggled a blueberry muffin out of the chow hall in my cargo pocket."

The creature slunk low to the ground and a snarl lifted his lip, bared his teeth, though no growl rumbled in his throat. It was all an act, false hostility. Really, the dog was frightened and unsure of this human looming out of the dark with his gunpowder smell, hard metal head, and clinking body gear.

Sergeant Morgan let the dog approach and eat the crumbled muffin out of his palm, then reached out with his other hand to stroke the bony head. The dog whipped around like he'd been hit with a tire iron, but rather than snapping off Rafe's fingers, he licked them.

"Looks like Sarge got himself a pet puppy," said Buckley.

"Hey, bud." Gerard made clicks and kissing noises with his tongue and lips to try and draw the dog away from the sergeant of the guard. "C'mere, bud."

But the dog stuck by Sergeant Morgan, nose batting around his cargo pocket for more muffin. "Hey," Rafe said. "Hey, hey, hey."

From that moment on, they went around like high school sweethearts.

The dog followed Sergeant Morgan, always at his heels. When we went for our morning runs, the dog was there, slinking like a coyote through the underbrush. When we went into the latrine for our showers, the dog sat outside staring at the door, ears cocked forward. When we went off the FOB for the day, the dog found a place to hide, usually in the shade-cool gravel beneath one of the trailers. When Rafe made his sergeant-of-the-guard rounds at night, the dog was by his side, squad mascot extraordinaire.

Right away we saw this was going to be trouble, because pets were forbidden according to General Order No. 1B. "Prohibited: adopting as pets or mascots, caring for, or feeding any type of domestic or wild animal," signed by those fat fucks in HQ.

When he first arrived on Taji, the dog hung back, head low to the ground. Its fur was patchy, bitten away in clumps, raw skin showing through. There was a dried scratch of blood on one of its hind legs. His rheumy eyes had leaked down the muzzle. If life under Hussein had been bad, this dog had been at the bottom of the pile of neglect. The zoo animals Saddam kept caged on his palace's hunting preserve in West Baghdad had had it better than this mutt.

Sergeant Morgan must have sensed this; we could see it in the way he leaned down and stroked the side of the dog's head. With every brush of the fingers, he pushed the Hussein years further and further into the past. We don't know about dog brains, but if it had been us, after what we'd already seen here in Iraq, nothing could have wiped away those memories, nice as Rafe's fingers might have been.

James Bond hung around the platoon area, tongue lolling as he stretched in the narrow bars of shade during the day while we were out on patrol. He'd come and go at random, somehow managing to cross the border between our FOB and Baghdad without being caught by the gate guards, but always staying at Rafe's side when he was with us, chilling after a long hard day. We fed him lunch meat from the dining facility and gave him sips of near beer, the nonalcohol the Army teased us with.

Those nights, the rest of us would distract ourselves with Xbox or dominoes or the latest issue of *Maxim*—pages wrinkled from the humidity of our masturbation—but Sergeant Morgan would always be playing with his dog.

"C'mere, boy." Rafe sat up on his cot and pulled James Bond to him, running his hands over the rib-thin body, grooming him with his fingers, pulling cockleburs from the fur. "Those badass hajjis treating you okay out there? Huh? Huh? You being a good boy for those terrorists?" The dog lifted his head and swiped a tongue across Rafe's chin. "You a good boy. Yes you are! Yes you *are!*"

We pretended not to notice, turning our heads. If Sergeant Morgan was unashamed to show affection toward this dog, his one true friend in all of Iraq right now, and if baby talk was involved, then so be it. We knew he'd nut kick any of us who made a wisecrack or arched an eyebrow in his direction.

James Bond laid his head in Rafe's lap and released a chuffy, muzzle-flapping sigh that said, *Peace on earth, goodwill toward men.*

Easy for him to say. The rest of us were out there in the shit every day, making nice with Local Nationals. Day in, day out. Beanie Babies and handshakes, long drives out to the provinces to deliver supplies to the latest school beautification project, pulling security as colonels sipped tea with sheiks. Days and days of driving, walking, and watching. Like Drew was fond of saying, "It sucked the dust off my granddaddy's balls."

The dog livened things up for a couple of weeks.

We taught James Bond to bark when the first sergeant and company commander approached, a signal we needed in order to stuff the contraband girlie mags back down to the bottom of our rucksacks. Nights when we got bored with the Sylvester Stallone DVDs and dominoes were no longer interesting, we watched the dog chase his tail like he was twirling an old European folk dance. We laughed because it was the stupidest thing in the world and stupid was all we had for entertainment in those days. Mostly, though, we liked feeling the lick of another creature's tongue on our skin. For some of us, it was the next best thing to having our wives by our side.

Even Snelling, a scout who *never* had anything nice to say about anybody, fell for the charms of the dog.

"Maybe we could learn the fuckin' mutt to start sniffin' bombs," he said one day as we sat around the Connex shipping containers we were calling home during this war. "Put him to work for us around here."

"He's doing enough as it is," Sergeant Morgan said. We could tell he didn't want to get all mushy over a dog in front of everyone else, but it was hard to keep the catch out of his voice. "He doesn't need to do anything else but be what he is."

"Oh? What's that?"

Rafe hesitated. "He's, uh, our mascot."

"I suppose," Snelling agreed.

"Yeah," Cheever piped up. "You don't see any other platoons around here with a dog, do you?"

"That's cuz all the other platoons smell like the inside of their mothers' cunts," Snelling said. "Who'd want to hang around *them*? Even a dog would roll over and play dead."

"Not just play dead, but *be* dead," Cheever said.

"Fucking A," Snelling agreed.

"Also," Rafe said, "there's that whole General Order Number One thing."

"That, too," Snelling said.

"Hey, Sar'nt, you ever think about what's gonna happen to your dog once we're wheels up and outta here?" This came from Buckley, who was second only to Snelling in the Department of Pessimism.

"Not really, Buckley. I'm just going day to day right now."

"Aren't we all?" Drew said.

"Hey," Cheever said. "We could try to smuggle him back to the States with us."

"Lotsa luck getting through customs."

"Yeah, no kidding," said Buckley. "We was at an inbrief down in Kuwait and they told us some lieutenant once tried to ship a baby camel back to the States. This dude had been at an outpost somewhere near the border and I guess he'd sort of adopted this camel and started treating it like his pet. So, when it comes time for redeploy, he and a few of his buddies put it in a Connex with some food and water. By the time it got back to the States two or three weeks later, and the customs agents popped that Connex open, hoo boy, that camel was pretty ripe. Like camel jelly kind of ripe."

Rafe pulled his dog closer in a one-arm hug. It was true. We hadn't thought about James Bond's future, but we sure as shit weren't gonna try a stunt like that. We'd rather see the dog keep roaming the streets of Baghdad than have him show up at Fort Drum all bloated with his eyes popped out and a gangrene tongue.

"Well," Rafe told us, "whatever happens, I'm just trying to give him a better life while we're here."

"You call that sour shit from the chow hall a better life?" said Snelling. "Jesus, it's a wonder he ain't been poisoned yet."

"Hey," Rafe said. "Nothing bad's gonna happen to him, long as I'm around."

"Sergeant Morgan, patron saint of hajji mutts."

"Fuck you, Buckley," he said with a grin. "Fuck all y'all."

"Yeah, fuck you too, Sar'nt." Buckley and all the rest of us grinning, too.

"Besides, James Bond here"—Rafe rubbed the sweet spot behind the dog's ears—"he's our good luck charm."

Howls of protest erupted from the men lounging around the shipping containers. "Oh, Sar'nt, tell me you didn't just say that!"

"He said it all right."

"Quick! Somebody unhex the jinx!" cried Cheever. "Sprinkle some virgin goat's blood in a circle around Sergeant Morgan!"

"The L word," Drew said. "Man, you know you *never* say the fuckin' L word. That's like eating a whole pack of Charms out of an MRE. Throw those fuckers away. Bad juju."

Rafe grinned. "Sorry. Must have lost my head for a minute." He grabbed the dog's muzzle and planted a brusque, manly kiss on the moist nose. "Still, you gotta admit, there's something about this dog."

"Yeah," Drew said. "I guess there is."

James Bond jumped to his feet, alert and bristling. He looked back at the platoon, then forward again. He started barking. We looked up, saw the company commander coming across the sand on his way to the row of porta-potties with a quick, mincing gait—like if he stepped too hard, something would jar loose. We all laughed, even Snelling.

"Hey," Buckley said. "We could give him to Hamid."

"Sure," said Sergeant Morgan. "How about it, Hamid?"

We looked at our interpreter, who'd been sitting some distance away. Hamid looked up, shrugged, grinned. "Maybe, yeah," he said.

We loved Hamid—almost as much as we did James Bond.

We knew next to nothing about his non-Taji life. Was he married? Did he still live with his parents? Did he have a hot chick of a sister? But what we *did* know about him was enough. He hated Coldplay, liked the first *Die Hard* but thought all the others were a waste of Bruce Willis's time, and chugged the tiny bottles of Tabasco from our MREs like they were tomato juice. ("You're a stud muffin, Hamid!" we cheered.) He was cool in ways we never expected a hajji to be.

Captain Bangor said he was the kind of interpreter you could trust to get the message right every time. "That Hamid is a stand-up guy," he'd said on more than one occasion; and Old Man Bang-Her is not one to go tossing around compliments.

Sergeant Morgan bonded with Hamid early on, just like he did with James Bond. They were what some hippy-dippy people might call kindred spirits. Maybe Rafe wrote something like that in an e-mail back to his parents. We don't know. All we know is the pair stuck together like glue on flypaper. Rafe taught Hamid American slang, and Hamid tried to school him on dance moves from his favorite Arabic pop music videos—which looked like a bunch of Bollywood bullshit to the rest of us, but we got a good laugh watching Rafe try to bust a move hajji style: shimmy sliding, whirling, and clapping his hands in sync with Hamid. They made a decent dance team. We liked to kid Sergeant Morgan about it, saying he should go sign up for the next Baghdad International Ballroom Dance Competition.

Once, shortly before they were both gone, Rafe said he had something for Hamid. He tossed a balled-up PX bag at him. When he'd untied the plastic handles and held up the black T-shirt, Hamid laughed and laughed.

"Let's see, dude," we said.

Hamid flipped the shirt around: I FOUGHT THE WAR ON TERROR AND ALL I GOT WAS THIS LOUSY T-SHIRT.

We remember Hamid was wearing that T-shirt the day Sergeant Morgan asked him if he'd take care of James Bond when we were gone.

"Sure, Rafe," he said. "Sure, I take care of him. I make sure he's good. With a nice barbecue sauce when I'm roasting him on the spit."

We laughed, though we weren't sure if Hamid was kidding or not.

Then one day, James Bond's girlfriend showed up.

"I found her outside my hooch last night," Sergeant Morgan told us, pointing at a new mutt crouched in the shadow of our trailers, haunches coiled, tense, ready to spring away. "I woke up hearing this whining and scratching at the door. When I opened it, JB flew out before I could get a hold of him." (Rafe was in the middle of his story, but we wanted to interrupt and say, "Wait a minute, now you're keeping him in your hooch with you?") "I thought I was looking at a fight for sure. Teeth snapping, fur flying. But it was nothing like that. JB went right up to her, sniffed her butt, then they started wrestling on the ground, making these weird groans, banging their muzzles together. That's when I realized she was his bona fide bitch."

"Or bone Fido bitch," Cartwright cracked.

Rafe said he realized that since he'd adopted James Bond as his unofficial pet, he hadn't allowed the dog to wander far. "I didn't stop to think he had a girlfriend waiting for him at home, worried out of her mind, wondering where he'd gone. I figure she tracked him all the way here, maybe digging a hole under the blast walls or—more likely—slipping past one of the checkpoints."

"Like something out of a movie," Miller said. "Love conquers all, or some shit like that."

"Yeah," Rafe said. "After all that, how could I possibly turn her away?"

We agreed she should stay here with James Bond and we swore we would keep it as quiet as we could, though we knew it was only a matter of time until First Sergeant or Lieutenant Grimner realized our new dog wasn't exactly a stray but the platoon's newest permanent resident. We hoped Top or Grimner—or both—would be in a good enough mood not to shoot our dogs on sight. So far, they'd been tolerant about letting us have James Bond—a tolerance that was affirmed when our turn-a-blind-eye battalion commander paid us a visit and didn't bust Sergeant Morgan's ass for violating General Order No. 1—but none of us knew how Top or Grimner would react when they saw this new unauthorized pet.

Skinner wanted to know what the girl dog's name was and Rafe said he hadn't thought of one yet. Santiago said he thought Esmeralda would be a good one but we shot that down as soon as it was out of his mouth. Holman said if she was James Bond's girlfriend, then she really needed to *be* James Bond's girlfriend. We tried to remember the movies and when all we could come up with at first was Pussy Galore and Octopussy, we knew those names would never work because it would be nothing but a constant reminder of what we couldn't have— and that if statistics were right, at least one of us would never see again. Miller, the platoon's self-proclaimed movie geek, suggested Holly Goodhead from *Moonraker*, but we all agreed that sounded too faggy, and finally Holman said the only Bond Girl he could remember was Halle Berry in the latest one and he thought maybe her name had been Jinx. And because we liked the way Halle Berry had risen out of the sea in her bikini, tits coming ashore a few seconds before the rest of her body, it was decided that Jinx it would be, all of us turning a blind eye to the implications of the name.

We always threw away our unlucky Charms. That should have been good enough.

We all agreed to smuggle extra meat out of the dining facility. Jacovich volunteered to let Jinx sleep in his hooch if things got too crowded at Sergeant Morgan's, but given Jaco-vich's questionable habits and his not-so-secret stash of porn, we worried for Jinx's health and welfare and so we ixnayed his offer of lodging.

When James Bond and Jinx, still playfully nipping each other, trotted around to the back of the Connexes, Jacovich laughed and said it looked like someone was gonna get him some Octopussy all right.

Then one of us said he saw First Sergeant coming out of his hooch and heading our way, so we scattered like we knew nothing, absolutely nothing, about a new dog in our midst.

That day, we went out on patrol in Sadr City, looking for weapons caches, roughing up a belligerent old man we thought was hiding AK-47s somewhere on his farm, kicking down doors throughout the day, killing two teenage boys who ran at us with machetes, and generally having a piss-poor time of it out there because of the goddamn heat and the never-ending dust. Whenever we looked at Sergeant Morgan, he seemed to be somewhere else, like he couldn't stop thinking about those two dogs. Like he couldn't wait to get off the streets and back to the FOB where he could sink his hands into velvet-soft fur.

Not too much later, came the bad day. The worst day yet for any of us. But especially for Sergeant Morgan.

We'd been on edge for hours, ever since Second Squad rolled out the door on their way to what looked like a major disturbance at Firdos Square.

"Trouble brewing," Lieutenant Grimner said. "S-3 says Mookie's whipping up his disciples into a frenzy. Effigies and the whole nine yards."

"*Burning* effigies, sir?" Cheever asked.

"Of course. What other kind is there?"

Rafe said nothing, but glared at a spot on the ground near the lieutenant's boots. Apparently everyone but Grimner knew Rafe's grandparents had had a history with the KKK back in the day, so fanatic Shi'a shit like this always put him off his game. It was like he had shards of glass in his mouth.

"Anyway," Grimner continued, "this shorthands us. With Second Squad out the door and most of Fourth on R and R, guess who draws the short straw? May as well get your heads in the game now. We're heading out soon. Mark my words."

There came the expected groans and a volley of curses. For Rafe Morgan, however, we could see the first thing that ran through his mind was: *Who'll watch the dogs?*

We'd been rotating dog-sitting duty between squads, everyone pulling their fair share of making sure the bowls had water and smuggling banana bread and saltines from the chow hall if everyone else was outside the wire. By now, James Bond and Jinx were the worst-kept secret on our end of the FOB. The CO, First Sergeant, and even Lieutenant Grimner knew the stray mutts had taken up permanent residence among us. Grimner didn't like it and we could practically hear General Order No. 1, subparagraph B ticking through his head every time James Bond trotted into sight, but Grimner was lower on the totem pole than the CO and if the CO ignored the dogs, then so be it. Which didn't necessarily mean James Bond and Jinx were riding home with us on the C-130; it just meant Rafe and the rest of us could enjoy their company for the remainder of our time in Iraq. Nothing more, nothing less.

But this had been Second Squad's week to watch the dogs and so now that left our squad to shoulder the task, and if we got called out (which, any minute, we knew we would), then it was up to the non-R&R-ing soldiers of Third Squad. But *they* were all pulling guard duty at the chow hall four times a day, so that meant the dogs were vulnerable to confiscation by the next ass-puckered sergeant major who came strolling by. It only took one senior fobbit with too much time on his hands to end our game of doggy hide-and-seek.

On that day soon after Jinx's arrival, a morning preluded with predawn explosions in the distant haze of Baghdad, things were blurred with confusion and misunderstandings right from the start. Bad things were going down in the streets beyond the concertina wire and by 10:00 a.m. everyone was walking around with hot pokers shoved up their asses, Second Squad was on its way to Firdos Square and Mookie's froth-mouthed fans, and we were up in the batter's box.

First Sergeant Weinz's poker was shoved up the farthest. When he screamed at us, we could almost see the metal tip in the back of his throat.

"First Squad!" he roared. "Get your shit and let's go. We got a live one. Baqubah. G-2 claims they found a nest of vipers and, lucky us, we get to go check it out."

Cheever ran past, intent on stuffing a thirty-round magazine into his ammo pouch, and almost collided with Jacovich coming at him from a ninety-degree angle. "Watch it, bitch!"

"No, *you* watch out for your own fucking self, asshole!"

The two ran their separate ways.

Weinz was screaming—volume turned up to eleven, veins popping and eyebrows nearly shooting off his forehead. The nine of us—Weinz was coming with us on this one—ran toward the armored personnel carrier. We zipped, we clipped, we strapped it all on, locked and loaded.

Sergeant Morgan was the last to head for the ramp, hesitating at the sight of JB and Jinx. "What about the dogs, First Sergeant?"

"The hell with the dogs," Weinz shouted. "Just get your ass in here, Morgan."

"But—"

"But *nothing*. I said fuck the dogs and I *mean* fuck, the, dogs!" Like every first sergeant worth his shit in the Army, Weinz knew when to bluster and when to coddle. We hated him and we loved him in equal measure and we never once thought about contradicting him. We knew his bite was just as bad as his bark.

Sergeant Morgan put his head down and mumbled, "Yes, First Sergeant." He ran up the ramp and Drummond levered it closed, sealing us into the small metal box. We shifted and settled on the benches. Drummond, driving, gunned the engine, threw the APC into reverse, and we jerked backward.

Then came a yelp and the unmistakable crunch of bone.

Someone started screaming, "No! Fuck no, *fuck* no!" It was Rafe. It was all of us.

The air was sucked out of the APC and our lungs withered. Even Weinz groaned when the realization hit him. He reached up and pounded against the hull for Drummond to stop.

Drummond levered down the hatch and we got out to look. Sergeant Morgan was the first to vomit, then two others turned and followed suit. From where the treads had ground the body into the dirt, a leg stuck up, quivering in the air, mere muscle memory at that point.

Rafe continued to heave until he came up dry, and then he reached out to grab James Bond, who was dancing and howling at the side of the APC. The dog sniffed the ground around what used to be Jinx. He lifted his head, gave an anguished yip, then let loose in a howl. This went on for some time.

Rogers from Third Squad ran over. He'd been resting in his hooch, on break between lunch and dinner guard shifts, when he heard the commotion. He stopped short of the crying, gagging bunch of us. "Fuckity fuck fuck!" he croaked.

"Rogers," Weinz said. "Get a shovel. Bury it. The rest of you, back inside. I'm sorry, Morgan, but we gotta get going."

We piled back into the APC, Drummond's hands visibly shaking as they took the controls again. Once again, Rafe hesitated at the edge of the ramp, holding a writhing James Bond by the scruff of the neck.

"First Sergeant—"

"Don't say it, Morgan. Don't even fuckin' say it."

"I gotta bring him, First Sergeant. I can't leave him here. I *can't*. You know that."

"Have a heart, First Sergeant," O said.

"I got more fuckin' heart than you'll ever know," Weinz growled at him, but we could see his face was fighting itself. We could see it even in the dim green light. Something tore diagonally across his brow, cheek, and jaw, and finally he growled, "Fuck it! Fine."

Rafe scrambled aboard, James Bond in tow. "Thanks, Top."

"But you better fuckin' keep that fuckin' mutt quiet or I'll have your fuckin' ass in a sling so fuckin' fast you'll be inside out before you know it."

"You won't hear a thing, Top. I promise."

We roared out of the FOB and shuddered our way up to top speed on the highway, racing toward Baqubah, our stomachs turning and clenching with every lurch of the APC.

Sergeant Morgan spent most of the trip rubbing James Bond's neck, trying to keep the whines from bubbling up, and whispering in the dog's ear, "It's fine. Everything's fine. Shh-shh. You'll be okay, boy. You'll be okay." Every now and then, JB's tongue came out and licked away the tears on Rafe's cheeks. "It'll be fine. You'll see."

And everything *would* have been fine, it really would have, if Drummond—jittery and distracted by the echo of bone crunch—hadn't taken a right instead of a left and then overcorrected by going two blocks too far and taking a left when he should have gone right, at which point the buildings, looming like stacked boxes, were determined to get him completely turned around and the next thing we knew we were heading down a dead-end alley. Drummond backed out of there only to take another wrong turn onto a stretch of road that looked like somewhere we'd already been, but turned out not to be, and then none of us—not even Weinz—had any clue how close we were to the alleged nest of vipers. When we called back to HQ and swallowed our embarrassment, admitting that yeah we were pretty fucking lost, HQ turned out to be no help at all because they'd lost track of the APC fifteen minutes ago and, as it turned out, the servers were down so they couldn't get a good fix on us. But stand by because they were doing their best to get everything back online as soon as possible. Just hold tight and don't go anywhere.

Weinz told Drummond to cut the engine and we sat there listening to the ticking metal. Holman, the gunner, kept swiveling, freaked out by the way the buildings seemed to be built completely out of nooks and crannies. We knew we shouldn't be this jumpy—we had the superior firepower, after all—but something about the way everything pressed against our faces like a pillow and the fact it was deadly silent out there, save for the grunting flap of laundry on an unseen line, yeah, we were pretty fucking unsettled by the current situation.

We sat and waited for HQ to come back to us. None of us spoke above a whisper there in the half dark. We sat tight against the benches, hands gripping our weapons, swallowing against the hammering of our hearts, flinching every time the laundry billowed or Holman hissed around the turret in another half swivel.

That's when James Bond wriggled free of Sergeant Morgan's hands, leapt to the space between the benches, and started to bark.

Rafe reached out and clamped down on the dog's muzzle with both hands.

Weinz hissed, "Shut him up *now*, Morgan!"

"I'm trying, Top. I'm trying." To James Bond: "Shhh-shhh-shhh. Dammit, boy!"

The bony muzzle took on a life of its own as James Bond thrashed his head from side to side, finding the strength to break free of Rafe's grip. The rest of us reached out, hands lunging into the green air.

The dog twisted and barked, finding an open spot near the back of the hatch where he could tip back his head and unleash a howl. Like the rest of us, his brain was probably still fogged with confusion, not understanding how and why Jinx had been sucked beneath the treads, exploding in a jet of blood, the musk of urine flooding his nose, and all he could do was howl, howl, howl.

We saw the glint of First Sergeant's 9 mm come out of its holster.

"No, Top, no!"

Rafe reached out and took the dog by the throat, squeezing, trying to press the howls back inside. The dog coughed, snarled, and once again slipped from his grasp and wheeled back and forth in the cramped confines of the APC, howling, howling.

"Either you do it, Morgan, or I do it," Weinz hissed.

"Top, Top, Top!" This was Skinner or O or Drew or maybe all three.

"Shut him up, Morgan!"

The dog, the dog, the dog. He wouldn't shut the fuck up.

Holman swiveled in half circles, freaked out by the commotion at his feet and the silence of the neighborhood.

James Bond barked and barked and barked. His eyes were wild, rolling with white half-moons.

First Sergeant held out the 9 mm to Sergeant Morgan, shaking it with insistence.

"Psst, psst, psst!" O tried to snare the dog's attention, distract him into silence.

James Bond threw himself from side to side, bouncing off the metal hull, acting like he was trying to bring the wrath of the neighborhood down on our heads.

"Morgan, I'm warning you for the last time!"

Rafe reached out to take the pistol. His head was floating over his body now, bobbing there in the green murk. This wasn't happening, was it?

Rafe tightened his fingers around the handgrip. He reached out for James Bond, and the rest of us put our fingers to our ears, none of us protesting now because we knew, all of us knew, down to the last man, this *had* to be done, it was just a fucking dog and none of our lives were worth losing over it. We hoped

Rafe would send the round deep enough into the dog that it couldn't ricochet out and kill one of us.

Sergeant Morgan gripped the neck fur between his fingers and pressed the barrel against James Bond's forehead. He couldn't look at those rolling eyes flashing their white moons, so he closed his own eyes. And then we all went deaf from the bang in the half instant before the blood splashed across us.

15

Fake Smile

We enter a marketplace. It is full of chatter and movement, people everywhere, but we pass through like ghosts.

We're ghosts because no one notices us. We walk past and they carry on, drinking their tea, reading their newspapers, babbling their conversations with fingers and tongues.

We pass a bookseller's stall full of magazines, laid out on a soiled rug. Bright, lurid covers full of celebrity faces none of us recognize. The Middle Eastern Tom Cruises and Kardashians. The Arabic words crawl across the faces like worms. One of the celebrities looks like Hamid, but we know this cannot be. Our terp was never anything but our terp. Still, the face on that cover has Hamid's smile.

The magazines are held down with fist-size rocks to keep them from blowing away. As they would from the wind of passing ghosts.

"Keep moving," Arrow says. Like he needed to say that.

*　*　*

They fished Hamid from the Tigris on the hottest day of our summer.

We'd given him a few days off to be with his family—something about his uncle coming to visit—and were doing our best to get along without him by improvising with ridiculous sign language, which did nothing but make the sheiks laugh.

All that morning we'd bitched about the triple-digit temps as we did a door-to-door in East Baghdad, trying to find patches of cool in the shade, yanking helmets off our throbbing heads, dousing them with bottles of tepid water. Nothing helped, nothing relieved. So by the time we pulled back into Taji at the still-broiling dinner hour, our throats were hoarse from cursing. We weren't hungry, but we went through the motions of standing in the chow line, letting them pile food on our trays, all the time impatient to reach the cooler of Gatorade bottles. We drank until our bellies were tight.

We heard about Hamid halfway through the meal when Thomasma from Third Battalion sat down with us and said, "Sorry to hear about your terp."

"What do you mean?" we said.

"You haven't heard?"

"No," we said, our furnaced skulls suddenly going chill.

Thomasma proceeded to tell us about the floating trash in the Tigris, Hamid facedown amid it.

About the rope with the grappling hook the police used.

About how they managed to snag him under his armpit.

About the hand-over-hand pull into shore.

About the bloat (which rhymes horribly with "float").

About the way Hamid rolled over in the water and seemed to smile up at the cops, until they realized that was just the gaping slit across his throat.

About how they dragged Hamid onto the sandy bank and the body had settled with gaseous burps in the afternoon heat.

About how Hamid was naked except for that stupid T-shirt Rafe gave him.

About how the Iraqi police had stood around in a circle, smoking cigarettes and trying to figure out what the caption on the shirt meant.

I FOUGHT THE WAR ON TERROR AND
ALL I GOT WAS THIS LOUSY T-SHIRT.

We listened to what Thomasma had to say, thanked him for telling us, then when he exited the dining facility, we followed and casually asked him to step around behind the building, where we beat the shit out of him.

16

Chicken

Now Rafe is dead, too, and we've got an appointment with his funeral.

We walk, we walk, we walk. Through the dust, through the thirst, through the sunbake, and now, through the Iraqis filtering into the marketplace with their goats, their dishdashas, their wind-flipped magazines, their snapping teeth, their cooking smoke.

Damn. Smell that?

We are hungry.

None of us had time to grab chow this morning before we stole the Humvee and none of us had thought to get an MRE from the backseat after it broke down. We are such idiots. And now our stomachs think our throats have been cut. (Sorry, Hamid.)

We push deeper into the marketplace. Skinned goats hang on ropes. Pyramids of pomegranates, figs, neon-yellow mangoes. Two men crouch over a grated fire, turning puddle-shaped slabs of flatbread with their bare hands. We can smell the sweet yeast and it drives us bat-shit crazy.

Arrow calls a halt, gathers us on a side street no bigger than an alley.

"Look," he says. "If we don't eat, we're gonna get ourselves shot. We're so distracted we can't think straight. Especially Cheever."

We look at Cheever. His lips are wet and bright.

"Time check," Arrow says.

Park pulls back his sleeve, then says, "Straight up noon."

"Shit," Arrow says. "That leaves us three hours."

"So we pick up the pace," Drew says. "We grab a bite to eat, then we head out at a double-time."

Arrow goes, "We're already at double-time."

"So we do triple-time."

"I think we need this," says O.

"Gotta feed the frame," agrees Cheever.

Cheever's frame doesn't need any more feeding. The rest of us on the other hand . . .

"Maybe there'll be food at the service," says Arrow.

"Fat chance," Drew says. "This is the no-frills Army, remember?"

"There won't be any food," Park says.

He's right. This wouldn't be like the time Cheever's Uncle George died and there were meatballs on toothpicks, pasta salads, cream puffs barely thawed because Cheever stopped at Costco on the way from the cemetery to the reception because he couldn't show up with nothing in his hands. It wouldn't be like the time O and his mother went to Denny's, just the two of them, directly after his father's graveside service and sat there looking at each other over the menus tacky with syrup and the paper placemats with a cartoon map of the USA—a tiny car stuffed with big-headed people, arms waving out the window, somewhere in Iowa—and neither of them knowing what to say because that cartoon family looked so happy, didn't it? And it would be nothing like the afternoon of Jernigan's wake back in Watertown when we'd all ended up at a sports bar raising a glass in honor of that stupid PFC we all loved before he went and got behind the wheel drunk. The bartender kept thanking us for our service, though none of us had been to Iraq at that point. We weren't about to let that stand between us and free drinks. We nodded, and said, "You're welcome." The beer kept flowing as we made up stories for the bartender about Jernigan and how he'd been like Medal of Honor brave that time in Ramadi. Man, did we have some laughs that night.

It won't be like that this afternoon at Sergeant Morgan's memorial service. No meatballs, no platters of sliced cheese, and for damned sure no beer. If we're going to feed the frame, it has to be here and now in this noisy, dirty, dangerous marketplace.

"Fine." Arrow relents. "Fine. But we pull security—three eat, three on overwatch. Got it?"

Fish, Park, and Drew are reluctant to give credence and credit to Arrow's new role as King Big Balls—no one and nothing but Sergeant Morgan's death elected him to that office—but he's all we've got at this point, so everyone shrugs, nods, and divides into two groups of three.

It feels like the street has gone quieter, like someone gave a half turn to the left on the volume knob as we move forward into the square. Eyes watch us. Hands flash secret signals at waist-high level. Women draped head to toe in flowing black garments part to let us through—like curtains pulling back in a theater.

That's right, hajji. We're America! Coming through, coming through. Step aside.

Arrow thinks this is nutso, but he lets it happen anyway. He's hungry as the rest of us. And *damn* if that chicken doesn't smell good.

The bird has been slow roasting all morning as we've made our way across this sector of Baghdad to make this date between fowl and appetite.

We form a ring around the men crouched over the fire. Drew, Park, and O are on the first security shift; Cheever, naturally, is the first to put his face into the smoke and say, "How much?"

The men at the edge of the fire are frightened. We can see that right away. They shift on their legs and look at each other. Can you blame them? Who wouldn't be edgy surrounded by a hedge of American uniforms prickled with rifle barrels and a fat kid drawing too near too fast. The men open their eyes wide and shake their heads.

We don't know if they're refusing to do business with us, or if they just don't understand Cheever's demand.

Arrow says quietly: "Kam thaman hada?"

The men look at each other, mutely signaling across the space of their squat. Then one of them, the younger one, holds up two fingers. What does this mean? Two dollars? Two dinar? Two minutes until the chicken is done?

"Hurry it up back there," O says.

"We're trying, man," Cheever says. "But hajji is being hajji."

"Okay, but we're starting to draw some attention here."

Arrow says something in Arabic to the men that must mean: "Hurry it up or we're leaving and taking our dinars with us." Because all of a sudden there is food in our hands—all of us, including the ones pulling security. Arrow nods and Drew, Park, and O go to sling arms.

Glistening muscle meat of chicken is cupped in soft, yeasty flatbread. Our noses fill with the scent of cloves, allspice, and pepper. The more food knowledgeable among us (meaning Cheever and O, who is a die-hard foodie back in the States) detect cardamom, coriander, and turmeric in the background of the aroma. We fold the blanket of bread around the meat and raise it to our mouths, as solemn as a communion service. We need two hands for the job: one to insert food, the other to catch juices in a cupped palm.

We bite into the chicken.

For nearly six months, we have subsisted on MREs and the slop at the dining facility. Cheddar cheese in a tube. Dehydrated peaches. Mystery-meat hamburgers.

Now, this marketplace food fills our mouths with clouds of flavor.

The crisp brown skin of the chicken crackles under our teeth, releasing the spices across our tongues. We think of backyard barbecues in Watertown, the camaraderie of beer and meat. We also think of perfumed tents in the desert, candlelit interiors piled high with pillows, a harem of half-dressed women serving us tea and platters of food. We lean back and open our mouths for grapes. Arabian Fucking Nights, man.

We take the food into our mouths and for a moment, on this saddest of days, it fills us with peace.

Even Fish—whose palms still sting from the jolt of rifle butt striking skull—enjoys the chicken.

We eat and eat and eat. We wipe our fingers on our pants legs and ask for more. The squatting men smile and say, "Good,

good"—or something like it in the local lingo. More food appears in our hands and we continue to gorge until we can't speak, only moan.

Cheever wants thirds, but Arrow reminds us of our timetable and, grumbling but nodding, we unsling our rifles and go back to port arms. We must move on.

We reach in our pockets and withdraw a linty mix of dollars and dinars. We toss the bills at the men and move out.

Cheever looks back. The men remain crouched, staring at the flutter of paper in the dirt, refusing to pick up the money, even after we are down the street and about to turn the corner.

17

Cheever

For Cheever, as you can imagine, food is the flaw—the unregulated, unchecked intake of calories that has only grown worse since his arrival in Baghdad. The dining facility's 24/7 buffet aside, we have watched Cheever tear into care packages—even ones not addressed to him, but left lying around the dayroom waiting for their rightful owners—casting aside the shampoo, the baby wipes, the greeting cards, and the Stephen King paperbacks until he found the cookies (homemade by housewives and children and now reduced to ziplocked baggies of crumbs), the beef jerky, the jelly beans, the potato chips (also reduced to crumbs during the transatlantic flights), and the ramen noodles. He'll leave the cellophane packets of microwave popcorn since he hasn't seen a microwave since he left Fort Drum, but he'll gather up the rest, a hunter clutching his bagged game to his chest with both arms, and make his way to his hooch, where he'll arrange the new food in his footlocker with as much care as a pioneer girl once packed her hope chest. He thinks the rest of the platoon doesn't know—but we know everything. We see him in the aftermath of hard missions, boot sore and head ringing from gunfire, as he goes first to his foot-locker to pull out not his weapons-cleaning kit, but a smooshed Twinkie. The rifle can wait; the crème filling cannot. Cheever is a food vacuum, sucking everything into the nozzle of his mouth. We're embarrassed when we go to the DFAC. We keep him at a distance, pretend he's someone from another unit stuffing his face up there. We tell others: Nah, we don't know that pudge holding out his tray for extra helpings of Salisbury steak and mashed potatoes . . . That's not our guy, the one piling on two slices of cheesecake, plate overlapping plate on the small tray . . . Cheever? Never heard of him. But yet, we'll watch him from the corners of our eyes as he sits in exile at the end of the table, ignorant of his ostracism as he plows into a ravenous gobble of steak, potatoes, cheesecake, buttered bread, ravioli, creamed corn, cheeseburger, quiche, soup, apple fritter, bacon, sausage, ham, and enchiladas. He is not a silent eater. He is a tooth clacker, a lip smacker, a finger licker. Once or twice, he groans like he's having sex. It all goes down the gullet in one big in-suck. We can hear threads on his uniform snapping from the pressure. Somehow, Cheever manages to maintain. For all his bulk, he keeps up with the platoon on morning runs around the FOB, never scores lower than 220 on his physical fitness test, passes all the body-fat measurements. Boot blisters aside, the lard ass doesn't slow us down and we are both astounded and angry at his success as a competent soldier.

18

Rafe Would Have Liked the Chicken

"I don't know if that was really chicken, but it was good," Cheever says.

"Damn straight," says Fish.

"Sergeant Morgan would have liked it," Park says.

"Yeah," we agree. We think of our platoon sergeant as we walk and scan, scan and walk, our eyes darting geometrically to sectors of vision, watching for the odd and out-of-place movement. We wonder: *Would Rafe be proud of us?* Or would he think we were fools for coming out here like this? We're not sure. Rafe was the kind of guy who could go either way. One thing's for sure: he would have liked the chicken.

Sergeant Morgan was by the book, lead by example, the field manual is my Bible one minute and a crazy fuck-the-FM son of a bitch with a wild hair up his ass the next. But that car chase through Sadr City back in March? That was a different Rafe. That 2.0 version of him scared the shit out of us.

We were responding to an incident that could have gone either way: boring as toast or high-body-count tragedy. We rolled off Taji clenching our jaws, our rifles, our bowels—anything clenchable. Sergeant Morgan was quiet, like something was eating him, but he didn't want to tell us about it. That was okay. We let Rafe be Rafe. Until, in one gunfire instant, he changed into someone else. *That* Rafe freaked us out.

We were answering a 911 from a convoy of contractors— engineering geeks from Harvard hired by the Army to come up with solutions for a better water system in north Baghdad. This pocket-protector squad had gotten themselves into a jam: ambushed in Sadr City, surrounded, fired on, SUVs set ablaze until the convoy was down to only one vehicle crammed with four surviving contractors, an interpreter, and three security sergeants from 3-1 who were doing their best to hold off the snipers.

We came galloping over the hill like the cavalry, heralding hope with our bugles (actually, we were just barreling through the streets, scattering women and kids with toots from our Humvee's horn). *Hold on, guys—we're on the way!*

We pulled up and, despite the three cars on fire and the smell of shit-filled underwear coming from the contractors' surviving SUV, the situation looked normal. No bullet blizzard, no brave-but-stupid Shi'a martyr tap-dancing toward the convoy with an AK-47 up to his cheek. By all appearances, this was just the aftermath of a single hasty attack.

A long line of backed-up cars needed to be checked and then funneled to side streets to get the traffic flowing again.

"We got this, boys," Sergeant Morgan said. We loved it when he called us "boys." Showed how much he cared for us.

We set up a perimeter, choking off pinch points north and south so no other cars could drive away until we'd checked the drivers' credentials.

Sergeant Morgan went up to the contractors—pale, sweating, and walking around like they'd just kissed death and lived (which they had)—and said it was cool: have a full team on-site soon enough to get everything towed away and cleaned up. Out of respect, he didn't say anything about the six charred bodies still smoking in the trail vehicles.

"Not a problem," Drew said to no one from where he crouched at his post along the line of waiting cars. "We got this. We guard these dudes until everything gets fixed and they leave and then easy peasy we're outta here."

He shouldn't have said that.

We weren't the only ones hoping to get out of there.

Sergeant Morgan's radar started pinging when he saw a black sedan do a three-point turn to extract itself from the bumper-to-bumper line of cars. The sedan lurched up and over the median and squealed away in the opposite direction.

It could be a harmless Local National—some guy already late for work and getting to the impatient "fuck this" point of hightailing it out of there. Or it could be the guilty party responsible for the attack, trying to blend in by hiding from us in plain sight, then getting freaked out when they saw Snelling and Cartwright work their way down the line, checking IDs and searching the trunks and undercarriages. It could be our bad guys trying to wriggle from the net, or it could be the proverbial innocent bystander.

This could go either way and we hated to abandon a perimeter to go chasing wild geese.

Our indecision blew away in a puff as Cartwright ran across the road toward Rafe. "Hey! Sergeant Morgan, those guys had guns! Four MAMs total and they all had weapons!"

Well, it wasn't some poor shmuck late for work after all.

We set off in pursuit of our MAMs—military-age males— leaving half the team with the shit-drawers contractors (who'd now added fear vomit to their playlist). They'd be okay until a team from higher headquarters showed up.

It was Sergeant Morgan, Cartwright, Drew, and O in one Humvee; Park, Buckley, Snelling and Hamid in the other. It took us four blocks to catch up with the black sedan. Traffic was heavy, which made it easy for us to see it ahead of us, snaking between slower cars and bouncing over curbs onto sidewalks. As we got closer, we saw the rifle barrels.

These Shi'a were anything but subtle.

We got close enough for the four men in the sedan to see us. The driver floored it, pulling away.

Oops, our bad.

"Go, go, go!" Sergeant Morgan banged on the dashboard and then keyed the mic to tell Park, who was in the lead Humvee, to glue himself to hajji's ass and stay there. Park pulled up and closed the gap.

After a quarter of a mile, the sedan hooked a sharp left at a gas station—too sudden for Park to follow.

Sergeant Morgan's Humvee squealed around the corner then roared ahead to catch up.

Park turned left at the next intersection, hoping to stay parallel with the rest of us.

The black sedan kept going faster and wilder, blowing through stop signs and squealing around corners, trying to shake us loose. We stayed right up on his ass, despite the extra weight of the Humvee. Cartwright knew what the hell he was doing.

We couldn't see Park at this point, but we figured he was out there somewhere and would rejoin us when it mattered the most. As it turned out, we didn't see that crew until we all regrouped on the FOB hours later.

The driver of the sedan gave it all he had and he was doing okay for a while since we had to pause at a couple of intersections to avoid hitting cross-traffic.

Then the sedan slowed and came to a stop in the middle of the street.

"Ha!" Cartwright crowed. "Fucker ran out of gas!"

We pulled up behind the sedan.

"No," Sergeant Morgan said. "I don't think that's it. Look at where we are."

We looked out the windows: on one side of the street, a church, on the other, a school.

It's like Rafe knew what was about to happen, like he saw the whole thing unfolding seconds before it happened. He frowned and started to say something, which got lost in what happened next.

Four windows rolled down, four rifle barrels poked out, four sparks of flame licked the air as automatic fire rang out.

Brr-rap! Brr-rap! Brr-rap! Brrrr-rap!

They weren't firing at us.

On either side, we saw people go down. A beggar holding out a paper cup in front of the church never had a chance. With quick surgery, bullets removed his hand. Coins flew up, then came down in a jingling rain. On the school playground, a boy flying high with giddy joy on a swing set jerked once and fell to the ground. We watched as bullets tore a girl in half, sending her severed body in opposite directions. We'll spare you the rest, but it was bad.

This all happened so fast none of us had time to react. We were numb, paralyzed, couldn't even feel the weapons in our hands.

The black sedan pulled away again, tires squealing with laughter.

Nobody said a thing. We had a choice to make: get out and help the living or take off after the bad guys. We wavered.

Sergeant Morgan was the first to break the silence. "Go!" he barked. "Go, go, go!"

Cartwright jammed his foot down, giving our Humvee everything it had.

We caught up. Drew was alive in the gunner's seat, firing bursts at the sedan, but not making contact because those fuckers were slippery, weaving from side to side. One of the passengers broke out the back window with the butt of his AK-47, then rested his muzzle on the shards and fired at us. Rounds hit the top of the Humvee and Drew ducked down inside for a second before popping back up and squeezing off another couple of bursts.

Cartwright kept up, bouncing us through the dips at intersections. This went on for several blocks, our weapons conversing in *brr-rap*s and iron-struck *ping*s.

We were still in a movie, but it wasn't fun anymore.

The whole time, Sergeant Morgan had this look on his face. It's hard to describe, but it was something like if a school bully had pulled down his shorts in gym class and that pissed him off enough to think about jumping the kid after school and punching his face until it turned to butcher meat. We'd never seen him so focused with the sole motivation of anger. He burned.

Eventually, the black sedan ran out of luck. When the killers tried to merge onto a four-lane highway, they hit a bottleneck at the on-ramp.

As we closed in on the sedan—whose taillights were blinking like a moth beating against a windowpane—all we could think about was that little girl they sliced in half on the playground. We had a new reason to finish this. The contractors were one thing, but this was a whole new territory of rage for us.

The sedan was slowed but undaunted by the traffic jam at the on-ramp. The driver found holes, places between cars where he could move forward, foot by metal-scraping foot. If we didn't do something, these guys would push themselves out and be free to speed away on the highway while our heavier Humvee hung back trapped behind the other cars. Some of the drivers had already pulled over to the side when they saw what was happening.

We were all shouting, "Shoot them! Shoot them!" But Sergeant Morgan tapped Drew on the leg and shouted, "No! Hold fire!" Then he turned to Cartwright and said, "Ram them." Cartwright hesitated and Sergeant Morgan grabbed the steering wheel in his left hand and growled, "Private, I'm giving you a direct order to ram their ass."

The guy in the back was reloading and looked like he wanted to treat us to a second go-round.

Drew slipped down out of the gunner's seat and we all braced ourselves against whatever we could and Cartwright leaped us forward.

It was like bumper cars at the carnival. The bad guys' heads snapped back as they were thrust forward. The sedan shot through a cleared path in the line of cars. Its back end was a crumpled mess—no match against the superior iron will of the American-forged Humvee. Can we get a *hoo-ah*?

We rammed them again. The sedan then took a half spin to the left and came to a stop. It was wedged between a silver SUV and a delivery truck hauling buckets of paint. One of the buckets tipped out, splashing red paint on the hood of the sedan.

We nosed forward until we were pressed against the sedan's front door. No escaping us now, motherfuckers!

We were within an arm's length of the sedan. We could have reached out and shook hands.

The men inside stirred and looked around at their options, which included bringing their AK-47s up off their laps.

Without another word, Sergeant Morgan opened his door, got out of the Humvee, and walked up to the sedan. His M4 was at his cheek. Rafe didn't hesitate.

Bam! Bam! Bam! Bam!

It was done. Four shots to four startled faces.

Drivers in the cars around us looked away. They wanted no part of this.

Sergeant Morgan got back in the Humvee, buckled up, then told Cartwright to get us out of there. That's all he said: "Let's go." Not another word the whole ride back to the FOB.

Fucking A. That was our Sergeant Morgan: breaker of international law, stoically doing the right thing. We were in awe.

When we got back to Taji and Buckley said, "Where'd you guys go?", we clamped our jaws and looked away. To protect Rafe, those of us in his Humvee kept mum about the whole thing. Tick a lock and throw away the key. We scrubbed the black paint off the Humvee's fender, made sure there were no telltale dents, and went about our business. If Sergeant Morgan had any thoughts on the matter, he kept them to himself until the day he died.

So, yeah, we think he would have blessed off on our car theft, our AWOL, our determination to make it through the city on our own.

Rafe would have liked that chicken.

19

Fish

Years before he entered the military, Fish killed a man and got away with it, no one ever discovering the body.

In Fish's opinion, the man—Charles Yardley—deserved every one of the eighteen stab wounds he got.

20

Nightmare

We dream of capture, of torture. We think about the slow death, flesh flensed from our bones in long strips with thin blades.

We're warriors, but we're also worriers.

The other night, Drew gnashed his teeth against his pillow, soaking it with drool, as he found himself in a dungeon lit by flickering torches. Very old-school Hollywood. Off in the distance, he heard the *squeal-screech-clang* of a heavy iron door closing and the echo of maniacal laughter.

Drew was strapped down to a metal table—or maybe it was stone. Whatever, it was cold against his back. He'd been stripped of his clothes. When he looked down the length of his body, it was like looking at a white sand dune, rising and falling, pocked with footsteps and furred with tufts of grass. He couldn't see his dick past the swell of his belly, but it was there somewhere (at least he *hoped* it was still there). What loomed largest in his vision were his thighs. They looked like hocks of meat hung in a butcher's window.

"Oh God, oh God," he groaned.

More mad-scientist laughter echoing through the dungeon's passageways. Then footsteps. Nearer and nearer and nearer.

The torches guttered and the light in the room dipped, winked out.

(In his hooch at Camp Taji, Drew drooled and chewed his pillow, tried to surface from the dream, but sank back to its depths.)

Dream blink. Change of scene. Now he really *was* strapped down on a metal table. Tissue paper crinkled under his body and he realized he was in a doctor's office. His feet were in stirrups and his knees were bent like he was about to deliver a baby. *Jesus!* He couldn't see his dick and he was pretty sure it was gone this time. Fluorescent lights buzzed overhead. Dead flies speckled the tubes.

"We have to take them, you know." A short woman old enough to be his grandmother stood near his feet. She wore a white lab coat and had a plastic face shield strapped to her head. She held up a circular saw. "The legs," she said in a sweet, cheery voice. "I'm sorry, but you know we have to take them."

Drew looked down the length of his body again. Someone had drawn dotted lines across the tops of his thighs with a marker.

"Do you *have* to take them?" he asked.

"I'm so sorry, sweetie, but you know we do. We've run out of options. They aren't coming for you."

"Can't we wait a little longer? Please? Please, I'm begging you!" Drew had never begged for anything in his life and he hated the whine in his voice as he cried out to the old woman.

"We're out of options. We're out of time." (What, were they in a fucking horror movie?) "The legs must go."

"Oh God, oh God."

"Bush called and said it was okay."

"What!"

"He called my boss and said it was okay, as long as we started with the legs."

(In his hooch, Drew's legs twitched and kicked, caught in the sweaty tangle of his bedsheets.)

"Oh Jesus God!"

The woman played with the trigger on the saw and the blade roared.

"You need to relax, sweetie."

Drew whimpered (he'd never whimpered about anything in his life) and he begged (again), saying, "Okay, okay, but can you give me something for the pain? Numb me up, bitch!"

"You know I can't." The woman shook her head. "You know it has to be like this." She revved the saw a couple more times—*rrr-arrr, rrr-arrrrr!*—and smiled as if that would have served as an apology. "Just relax and it won't hurt as much. I'll try to be quick." She flipped the face shield down.

"Wait! Wait!" Drew screamed.

The saw stopped and the woman looked up. But now she wasn't somebody's grandmother. She was younger and Middle Eastern—beautiful as a supermodel. And she no longer spoke English. She unleashed a tide of angry words that crashed around the room. The only word Drew recognized was "Allah."

The woman bent over Drew's legs and prepared to go to work. The saw had disappeared from her hands, replaced by a rusty butter knife with tiny serrations at the tip.

This was going to take a long time.

The woman smiled at Drew, this time without sympathy. She had bright white teeth. They were sharp as razor blades.

He screamed himself awake as the butter knife bit into his skin.

That dream had come to Drew three nights ago—a premonition for today's unexpected march across Baghdad.

God, his legs hurt so fucking much.

21

Legs

Thigh, knee, calf, ankle, heel.

Hamstring, gluteus, quadriceps, dorsal flexors, and sartorius—the longest muscle in the entire human body.

It's a factory down there.

Our legs are levers.

Our legs are wheels and pistons and pulleys and cogs.

Our legs are shock absorbers.

Our legs are gazelle springs.

Our legs are giraffe stalks, taking long skittery strides.

Our legs are meat and muscle, shanks of ham and lamb and beef.

Our legs are tree trunks and blades of grass.

Our legs are made of water and wind.

Our legs are two fingers walking across a table.

Our legs, our legs, our legs are the only thing we believe in anymore. Our legs will deliver us from all evil. Our legs, who art in heaven, hallowed be thy name.

22

One Foot in Front
of the Other

Once upon a time, Cheever almost got himself blown up. This was years ago, in a different place, a different unit—long before we were "we."

Back then, Cheever wasn't a Signal soldier attached to our infantry unit. He was the lowest of the lowly fobbits: a Public Affairs pogue who spent the majority of his time inside airless headquarters buildings lit by flickering overhead fluorescent lights. His job was to write stories—fluffy and sweet as a bowl full of marshmallows—about Officers' Spouses' Club scholarships, new books at the post library, and the occasional movie review for the post newspaper. Hardly anything about quote unquote real soldiering. The only times he got out of the office were to interview people like the corporal in Finance who had won some award for his stamp collection or to ride along with animal control MPs who cruised the post picking up stray cats, dogs, and—once—a purportedly rabid raccoon. The rest of the time, Cheever sat in his small, dimly lit office rewriting the police blotter so it came out kind of funny and surfing lingerie websites—the closest thing to porn allowable on his government computer. He lived on bags of Cheetos and Costco-size boxes of Twinkies he kept in his lower right-hand desk drawer. You think he's fat now, you should have seen him back in the day. Every six months at the conclusion of the Army Physical Fitness Test, he'd find himself standing in stocking feet in the company commander's office as an NCO ran a tape measure over his doughy flesh, calculating his body mass index and jotting numbers on a form pinned to a clipboard. How Cheever passed those APFTs and survived long enough to make it into our platoon is beyond us. Dumb luck, we figure.

Speaking of "dumb," this brings us to our story.

So there he was—Cheever—three years ago on a training exercise in Thailand. To his horror, he'd been yanked out of his soft, safe garrison routine and attached to an infantry company that was going to the jungles on the border of Laos for a month to share training tactics, techniques, and procedures with members of the Royal Thai Army. Cheever's job was to take large numbers of photos—battery-draining quantities—and e-mail them (along with five-hundred-word stories) back to the post newspaper, where some other Twinkie-stuffed private would edit the story and lay it out in that week's edition.

All well and good—and, in fact, Cheever was kind of getting into it, despite the heat, the khao phat that gave him the watery shits for a week, and rumors of a tiger prowling the hills above the city. He was digging the excitement of this adventure, losing himself in the photos he artfully arranged in his viewfinder. Eventually, he'd return to the comfort of garrison air-conditioning and junk food, but for now, he went along with this mission like he really cared about the Army.

One afternoon, when the grunts were busy in the barracks cleaning their rifles, Cheever wandered into the city, camera in hand.

He passed auto repair shops opening onto the street, the whir of pneumatic drills coming like sexual moans from deep inside the garages. The heavy air carried the sizzling smell of frying chicken. He passed stacks of dried fish (fins and eyeballs and scales included). His throat was lined with the harsh aftertaste of motor exhaust, a bitterness that burned his esophagus. He was already sweating and his skin was throbbing and every time he passed one of the street-side food vendors another wave of smoky heat beat against him. The vendors cooked on portable propane ovens right there on the curb, glass cases on either side of them filled with skinned chickens, spits of marinated meats, and beds of dirty ice on top of which sat fresh vegetables (white, root-like, gnarled like deformed knuckles) and giant prawns and mussels. Cheever raised his camera and clicked and clicked and clicked. He walked along the sidewalk and threaded his way among the tables and chairs set up in the middle of the throughway, trying not to bump into them with his oafish American body. Old men sipping their soup and slurping their fried noodles stared at him muttering "farang," and the young Thai girls covered shy giggles with their hands when he glanced in their direction. He walked on past another engine shop where a young Thai man, stripped to the waist, was peeling a tire off its rim. At his side was a urine-colored dog, half its fur eaten away by disease, its head so listless and lazy that it could not lift it from the sidewalk as Cheever passed. He walked on past a shop selling fans and stereos and compact disc players, all shrink-wrapped in plastic and overpriced. He walked on past another vendor smelling of grease and ginger and the musk of seafood, past a coffee shop called Al Pacino Cappuccino and a place called Giant Big Man Club. He walked on past a building where water from an upper-story air-conditioning unit dripped on his head and shoulders.

Eventually, he arrived at a zoo full of skinny, flea-bitten animals. He paid his admission and walked slowly through the exhibits, raising his camera and trying to get some decent shots between the bars. He saw white-handed gibbons (one of whom reached a long hand through the cage and slapped Cheever's head as he tried to take a picture), flamingoes, a large black squirrel, and a herd of Eld's deer, which resembled the small whitetails back home in Pennsylvania. They had glistening purple-brown noses and magnificent racks chandeliered over their heads. There was a newborn fawn that couldn't have been more than a few hours old; the mother was still licking it. Its hooves were the size of licorice bites, legs shaped like dowels and thighs still pressed together in memory of the birth canal. He's not sure why, but standing there in front of that cage, staring at this fresh, still-slick deer, Cheever began to cry. Then he got mad at himself for the tears and leaned forward and banged his forehead several times against the rusted bars until the mother deer got nervous and began to bleat like a wounded lamb. That night, Cheever sat on his cot in the barracks and deleted every photo of the city he'd taken that day. He wanted to be out of this country, out of the Army, out of this life altogether.

Wait—this isn't the story we want to tell. Sorry, we got a little distracted by the sight of Cheever, the stupid tub of lard, getting slapped on the head by a monkey. *Here's* the story:

On the third week of the training exercise, before his visit to the zoo, Cheever and his company of infantry soldiers were visiting a Thai military camp; it was the host nation's turn to show the Americans what Thai training was like. Most of it involved walking through the jungle, bending to examine broken branches and boot-crushed leaves, a long, involved ceremony that ended with everyone bowing and chanting "ommmm," and catching three-foot snakes by hand, snapping their heads with a two-handed twist, then gutting, roasting, and eating the flesh.

Before that dinner theater, however, everyone gathered around a large plot of freshly turned soil—about the size of a Hollywood swimming pool—as three Royal Thai Army soldiers gave a demonstration in "route-clearing procedures." The company's first sergeant, kindness in his heart, ordered the American soldiers to take off their uniform tops and strip down to their sweat-soaked brown T-shirts, but to keep their helmets on, chin-straps tightened. He didn't want to embarrass the United States with heat casualties. Everyone sat cross-legged around this pool of plowed earth, drinking cool bottles of water and watching the Thai soldiers move across the dirt, sweeping metal detectors in front of them and listening to the clicks that came through the headphones clamped tight against their ears.

A Thai colonel stood off to one side narrating their actions in broken English: "Now he step one foot, one foot . . . Now he listen for *click-click* . . . Now he go three step left, two step forward."

Cheever was frustrated. He was at the back of the crowd, at a bad angle to get a decent photo. He tried holding his camera over his head and clicking off a few frames, but when he scrolled through them on the digital display, they all looked like shit.

He'd gotten the backs of the Americans' heads, but the paper back home needed *faces*. The only way to get that was to go on the other side of the Thais and shoot back toward the US soldiers.

He made his way around the edge of the formation and stepped into the cleared field. The soil beneath his boots was soft as pillows. He was halfway across and about to raise the camera to his eye when everyone erupted in a jumble of yells: "Hey! Hey! Hey!" and "Stop! Stop!" and something in Thai he couldn't understand. Cheever shrugged, thinking it was part of the demonstration. He fired off a few shots—all the soldiers were waving at the camera—but realized he needed to get a little closer to be able to see faces in the photo. Everyone was still yelling and now there was clapping. The Thai minesweepers had stopped and turned to look at Cheever. He'd taken another three steps when he heard the deep bellow of the first sergeant: "PAO—freeze!"

Cheever wasn't a regular part of this unit, so no one really knew his name. To them, he was just the job title, Public Affairs. So when he heard "PAO!" fired across the field, Cheever suddenly realized the crowd had been yelling at *him*.

Across the field, everyone—including the Thai colonel—was waving their arms like semaphores. Now he heard the words: "Get off! Get off!" "Mines! Mines! Mines!"

Cheever froze. His balls tingled, rotating through his sac. His mouth filled with cotton.

He looked around him at the black clods of earth. He saw red flags sunk in the soft dirt at irregular intervals and suddenly he knew what they were for, what they marked.

Sweet Jesus God, have mercy on me, your humble, idiotic servant.

Legs trembling, he stepped backward, trying to place his feet in his own boot tracks as he made his way off the minefield.

When he reached the rest of the soldiers, they were on their feet and looking at him like he was the stupidest piece of shit on earth. More than a few were shaking their heads and cursing him for making the rest of them look bad.

"Sorry," Cheever said with a weak grin.

"Sorry?" the Thai colonel said, frowning. "You sorry?" He picked up a fist-size rock at his feet. "Here your 'sorry.'"

Cheever flinched, expected the colonel to bean him over the head. Instead, he turned and flung the rock in an arc over the field. It landed in a spot near where Cheever had been standing, blithely taking photographs.

Ka-whoom!

An earth geyser shot twenty feet into the air, raining bits of soil on Cheever standing, openmouthed, fifty yards away.

23

Park

Park is our quiet one.

Park holds it inside. He is a balloon: the air escapes by small, slow degrees. So much pressure behind that knot.

In this, he is much like his grandfather. He fought in the old war. On the Korean side. Against Americans like Sergeant Morgan, Arrow, Cheever, O, Drew, and now Park himself. Grandfather didn't talk much about his time in combat. He died before Park's war, so what he'd think of us over here, pushing our way into these desert cities, will stay a mystery. Grandfather built a retaining wall inside himself and stayed behind it. He was a quiet one.

As a boy growing up in Los Angeles, Park was close to his grandfather, trailing behind him on nights and weekends—grade-school footsteps inside the old man's larger ones—walking along the pier, flying kites, or watching Grandfather carve his animals, the blade growing out of his thumb, his thumb peeling the wood, the wood revealing the four-legged bodies. The two of them seldom discussed the grandfather's past, his cold months in the mountains taking aim at bundled, huffing Americans climbing upslope. But when they did, the old man would say things like: "War is nothing but the dead fighting the dead" or "I once found a hand—just a hand—in a snowbank. White and beautiful as marble. A piece of statue. It was the worst thing I saw during that war." Beyond that, his grandfather remained clammed and dammed. Nothing out, only in.

Park practices his ways. Stoic as statuary.

So, that night onstage with the Country Bumpkins at Taji two months ago? It nearly killed him.

We were drunk on enthusiasm and near beer. These MWR Fun Nights were our release. Our morale and welfare needed some recreation, all right. At concerts, we packed the PX courtyard with our beige bodies, filled the night air with our cheers. The bands were never big names—only rising stars and falling has-beens—but they were good enough for us, the entertainment-starved.

None of us had ever heard of the Country Bumpkins, but that didn't matter. For the space of two hours, we loved those three girls with their straw hats, their breasts, their smiles.

We were carried away by the night, the near beer, our need for something other than this war.

Sergeant Morgan was the one who pushed Park forward, goaded him to go up there, ordered the rest of us to lift him above our heads like he was some tribal sacrifice we were about to throw in a volcano.

Park protested. He struggled against our grip. He wasn't into this shit.

He pictured his grandfather shaking his head, casting his eyes down to the floor. Such noise, such loss of dignity.

Then Park was onstage, lifted up and over the front barriers, wrists yanked by the band's security team. He was surrounded by the trio of big-haired girls in denim cutoffs, their shirts—*holy mother of God!*—little more than checkered hand-kerchiefs wrapped around their chests and knotted behind their necks, barely holding back breasts swollen with silicone. Park pulled his gaze away quick as he could, but it was too late. The crowd had seen him ogling the boobs and now everyone had their O'Doul's-oiled throats wide open: roaring, leering, chanting.

Park glanced over at the bass player—a beefy dude in a straw hat, shirtless beneath a pair of overalls—and got a thumbs-up and a wink.

Park wanted to die. He prayed his grandfather's ghost would send a mortar whistling through the sky to land bull's-eye here on this stage.

"We're gonna need a little help with this next song," one of the Bumpkins said, looking out into the crowd. "What do y'all think? Think we can persuade—uh, what's your name?" She put the microphone against his mouth.

"Park."

"Park," she said. "Don't tell me. Lemme guess: they call you Private Parking, right?"

Our laughter nearly toppled the walls of the courtyard.

Park's face was marble. Hard, impenetrable.

"Sorry, I couldn't resist." The Bumpkin bitch wrapped her arm around his shoulder. "What's your first name, darlin'?"

She held the microphone to his lips like it was a lollipop she was offering him. Park looked at it like it was a dick she wanted him to suck.

"The strong, silent type, huh?" She giggled.

Then Park did the incredible, the unexpected: he told her his name.

"Lee—that's a nice name," the girl said. "I had me a boy-friend once named Lee. Wadn't as cute as you, though. Besides, I think he loved his coonhound more'n me. Gladys—that's the dog—used to drink Coors straight out of the can. One day, I up and told Lee he had to choose: me or the dog. And so that's what he done. Last I heard, he 'n' Gladys were living happily ever after in a double-wide in Tulsa." Behind them, the drummer snapped off a rim shot followed by a bass-drum kick.

Park begged the stage to collapse and bury him.

"All right now!" the girl called to the crowd. "Y'all think we can persuade Lee—*this* Lee, our all-American *hero* Lee—to join in on the chorus?"

"Hell, *yeah*!" came the response. Park heard Sergeant Morgan's voice the loudest among them: "Go, Park!"

We stood at the front, cheering him on. Those of us who had lighters flicked them on, waved them above our heads.

The three girls led Park center stage. Their breasts squeaked when they walked. Even through the roar of the crowd, Park could hear the silicone.

They put that lollipop-dick microphone in his hand and slapped a Styrofoam cowboy hat on his head.

Americans. He hated every last goddamn one of them.

The tallest of the Bumpkins nodded over her shoulder to the band and they started in on "God Bless the USA."

A groan rose from the courtyard. Not *that* song. We were all so sick of "God Bless the USA" by that point, a little puke came up in the back of our mouths every time we heard the first words of the swampy, patriotic treacle. If we ever saw Lee Greenwood walking down the street, we'd kick the ever-lovin' red-white-and-blue shit out of him.

But these girls didn't know any better. They were really into it.

Closed eyes. Glitter-dusted hair sparkling in the spotlight. Harmony. Patriotism. Sincerity. The girl with the big hair opened her lips and started to sing.

Park wanted to puke. When one of the Bumpkins pushed his hand holding the microphone to his mouth during the chorus, he thought he'd be better off belting out Barry Manilow's greatest hits than he would the most hated song in the military. But the girls had stepped aside, leaving him center stage with the microphone. Park looked over. Were they—? Oh my God, yes they were. The Bumpkins were marching in place and saluting him like he was some hero in a small-town parade.

When he didn't start singing, the band petered out and looped back to the beginning of the chorus.

Park shook his head.

"He needs some encouragement, y'all," one of the Bumpkins called to the crowd. "Come on, let's make some noise for Private Park!"

Some joker hooted out from the crowd, "Yo, he can't get it up! You're in a no parking zone!" That set off a wave of laughter—from everybody but our small squad standing at the front edge of the crowd, all of us now sorry we'd crowd surfed him onto the stage.

Drew turned and shouted back into the crowd: "Shut the fuck up!"

Park thought: *Here's your loss of dignity, Grandfather.*

The band looped back for a third try at the chorus. One of the Bumpkins, getting exasperated with him, began to softly sing. She raised her eyebrows and rolled her hand in encouragement. "Come on, we'll help you with the words."

Park shook his head again and dropped the microphone, which landed with a mortar-loud *boom*. Then he walked to the front of the stage and jumped back into our arms. We tried to pat him on the shoulder, tell him sorry, but he threw us off. There was a look in his eyes that made us step back from him.

Rage. Sure, Park has pent-up anger. It lurks in him like a hissing, wheezing forty-year-old boiler in the basement, bolts corroded with rust, seams leaking water, gauges no longer reliable, ready to blow any minute. *Evacuate the house, everyone!*

Park comes by his pissed-off nature honestly. It's in the DNA passed to him by his grandfather, who never quite got over the wrongs he suffered in the cold wastelands of the 1950s. *That beautiful, finger-curled hand was the worst thing I ever saw.* Park learned to hate America at the knee of his grandfather—even as he was filling his lungs with American oxygen, buying American video games at American malls, absorbing American cartoons, and gorging on American burgers with cheese, fries, and strawberry milkshakes. The more of America he took in, the greater his rage grew—gas to the rickety boiler.

But all this anger had nowhere to go. Park knew he had three options: he could stuff it inside and close the lid, he could let it go, or he could channel it. He chose the first option.

Unlike Fish, who expressed his feelings by plunging a knife into another man's body, Park did not resort to violence. At least not toward anyone else. But the landscape inside him was barren and black: scorched earth and smoldering tree stumps.

Park walks quiet among us. We don't hear him screaming and sweeping his flamethrower across the path in front of him.

24

Bride

We've gone another half mile when an unseen dog takes up a broken-record bark. One yip after another after another after another. Almost like it's saying, "Hark! Hark! Hark!" We think of James Bond and some of us—the more superstitious ones—wonder if it's a canine ghost warning us away from the neighborhood we're about to enter.

We pass a soccer field: open ground, a vacant lot choked with weeds and paper trash on one side, low-lying buildings on the other. Ahead of us, the street curves past mosque turrets. Farther still, on a small rise in the distance, a stone arch, dating back to ancient Persia, shoulders through a forest of billboards and glassy buildings, defying its centuries of crumble. It's all more of the same Baghdad beige we've seen for six months. Nothing out of the ordinary. Except that dog.

We enter the business district and spread ourselves along the street. We get our distance, not bunching up. We hug the walls of the stores, slipping into the shade with sighs, but not allowing the ten-degree difference to distract us. We walk with

our rifles at the ready, trigger fingers poised for action. We stir
a haze of dust as we advance through the thickening crowd of
Iraqis. The market is black with abayas, white with dishdashas.
The air gurgles with tongues, voices that sound more like singing than talking. Behind us, the dog has stopped barking. Or
maybe we just can't hear it anymore.

"Jesus," says Drew. "Look at all of them. There's too many."

"Easy, easy," says Arrow. "Let's play it cool here. We're just
another law-and-order patrol. They see this all the time."

"We're cool," says Drew.

Park goes, "We real cool."

Men, women, and children watch our approach. The air
dust sparkles and makes the locals look fuzzy, out of focus. The
older Iraqis, those who spent decades in Saddam's "correctional"
facilities, smile at us with stumps of rotten teeth. They sip their
bitter coffee and sweet chai and nudge each other. When they
wave, we notice many of the hands (if they aren't outright missing) have only three or four fingers. The women keep their eyes
averted and go on with their shopping, chatter-singing at the
men selling meat and vegetables, bargaining for the best price.
The younger men—military-age males, the MAMs we're always
targeting—stare with undisguised hatred at us, the intruding
infidels. This is Sunni territory and most of them have grown
weary of the American presence and, in the cases where rela-
tives have been killed by soldiers firing at cars that approached
checkpoints too quickly, have lately felt the slow simmer of
anger come to a boil. The children, as usual, skip along beside
us chanting, "Mister! Mister!" Waiting for that happy moment
when one of us reaches into his ammo pouch and comes out
with a ziplock baggie of Jolly Ranchers.

That's us. We're jolly ranchers, herding the bleating kids along the street. *Baa-baa, la-laa, Mister, Mister!* All we need are dogs like James Bond and Jinx nipping their heels to keep the rug rats in line.

Then we're all sad and shit because we have no candy and because we've remembered the dogs. And the dogs lead us back to Sergeant Morgan.

We shake it off. We ignore the wavers, the haters, the beggars. For all they know, we're just a bunch of dudes on patrol. They see this all the time. We sweep our eyes over the crowd, darting into every nook and cranny and rolling upward to the top-floor windows, a visual circle that clicks like a checklist inside our heads. We are focused, laser intent on the mission. Get through the marketplace like a shaft launched from a bowstring. We're all arrows.

Out of our way, motherfuckers. We're coming through! America Big Boots will stomp you flat if you get in our way. We wait for no kid. We pause for no mister.

We pass a beauty salon. Some of us, our knees go weak when we slow long enough to stare through the plate glass window. There, under Hollywood-bright fluorescent lights, stands a bride being primped for her wedding. Her veil, her dress, her gloves—they're so dazzling, some of us have to squint to keep from going blind. The salon is brighter than the sun on the street.

This bride, this *vision*, stands in the middle of the beauty salon, surrounded by a half dozen other women in black abayas. These ladies-in-waiting, these dark bridesmaids, they're moving around the bride—checking the hem of the dress, fluffing the veil, nipping, tucking, smoothing. They are ravens pecking for seeds around a radiant dove.

We can't hear anything through the window, but we guess the beauty salon is full of chatter, and the hiss of a hair dryer, and the rhythmic scratch of a fan in the corner. We know one thing for certain: the bride is laughing. We see that, plain as day. In our minds, we hear the coin jingle of her throat. We feel the warm breath coming from her lipsticked mouth, the cherry-red lips we want to press against ours, the mouth we want to taste and by which, in turn, we want to be swallowed. It is beauty, it is light, and we are stunned right down to our rubber knees.

And on this day, in this month, this year, this too-long slog of days upon days filled with dust and death, the routine of numb and dumb, the spikes of adrenaline, the scattered parts of Sergeant Morgan, the heat, the iron scent of blood, the grime coating our faces—*all of it*—on this day, we need this bride, this razzle-dazzle of light behind plate glass, this singular hope.

We remember something Hoover, the chaplain's assistant, said not too long ago: "Did you know the number of marriage licenses issued in Baghdad is double this year over what it was last year?"

"No shit?" we said (we always took every opportunity to swear around chaplain's assistants—though they usually gave as good as they got).

"It's all due to the collapse of the Ba'ath Party," Hoover said. "For years, they controlled who did and didn't get married, but now that they're gone . . ." He made a crumbling motion with his hand. "It's a free-for-all out there. A real fucking party of joy."

We don't have time to do much more than crane our necks, slow to a giddy wobble, before pushing past the beauty salon. Arrow is moving out at a rapid pace. He hasn't seen—or hasn't wanted to see—the bride. His neck is stiff; his eyes are fixed on a point ahead of us.

We want to call out, "Hey, Arrow, wait up, will ya?" But our voices die to a croak on the "hey."

It's no good. Arrow won't wait. This is no party of joy for him today.

25

Wedding

There was that wedding reception we'd attended not too long ago. We were late, uninvited. Wedding crashers. By the time we arrived, things were a mess.

As we walked through the rubble, the craters, and the splashes of blood, Hamid reconstructed the scene for us, based on what he'd gathered from the neighbors and kids on bikes who still hung around the scene even after we arrived in our Humvees.

"The groom was a law student at university," Hamid said, voice husky from the smoke—or sorrow. It was hard to tell. "The bride, she was the only daughter of the president of a furniture company. Very wealthy man. Made big money in desks and chairs in the 1970s and kept it, even through the Saddam years. Now, he's doing—*was* doing—big, big business selling to US Army headquarters coming in to Baghdad, setting up their offices."

Sergeant Morgan looked at him, frowning. "Those kids told you all this?"

"Yes—but, no, I also know the man," Hamid said. "Know him through newspaper stories. Like I said: very, very rich. This wedding was—as you Americans say—a really big deal."

Sergeant Morgan knelt beside an overturned metal platter of food, a spill of rice coming from beneath in a delta. He touched the plate—as if to turn it over—but yelped and jumped to his feet, shaking his fingers. The tray was still hot, long after it had been seared by flame.

"So how did we get from 'I do' to this?" he asked Hamid, sucking his fingertips.

"Wedding was this morning. They start early because it lasts all day. It was all very happy, all very good. Cheerful—laughing, singing, some dancing. Then they all came back here to the house of the bride's family for the walima. Feast. You know 'feast'? Is that the right word?"

"Yeah, like a reception," Sergeant Morgan said. "I get it."

"In our country, men and women they don't eat together," Hamid said. "Men eat first, tell stories about the bridegroom, laugh some more, maybe drink too much. Then the women eat, indoors, away from their husbands and fathers. Not as much drinking, but still lots of stories. That is how I think this one went today, how I see it in my head." Hamid, the fool, was getting all misty-eyed and choked up.

He and Sergeant Morgan stepped around a body part as he continued to narrate the scene. "Then, after the proper time has passed, the groom comes to the women's feast—he is shy and maybe embarrassed—and everyone toasts the couple with orange soda."

"Orange soda?" Rafe asked. "That's the tradition?"

Hamid shrugged. "Maybe they drank Diet Coke here. I don't know. At my cousin's wedding, it was orange soda."

"Go on," Rafe said. "Then what happened?"

"Then there was more dancing. Everyone's together now. Men, wives, children. The very rich father, he's hired a band, so musicians are playing loud and with happy excitement. Drums, trumpets, cymbals. The bride and groom are in the street, holding hands, swinging each other around and around in circles." Yep, no doubt about it: Hamid *was* crying. We could see that from where we were doing our work—pulling security, measuring craters, and marking the groom's body parts with circles of spray paint.

Hamid pulled a once-white handkerchief from his flak vest. He wiped his face. "This goes on into the night, all the way to dawn. Finally, a neighbor gets tired of all the trumpets. He comes out yelling, firing his rifle straight into the air. Nobody stops. They hear him, but nobody stops. The joy, it is too great. The neighbor, he's still mad, but he goes back inside. Or maybe he gives up and joins them in the street. The kids I asked weren't too sure about this. About an hour later, a mortar—maybe two, maybe three—lands here in the street and—and—" He can't finish. Hamid is done. The handkerchief is flying like a flag from his face.

"Three, by the looks of it," Rafe said. And *damn* if there isn't a catch in *his* throat now, too.

The rest of us, we look away. Sergeant Morgan would shit a brick if he caught us watching him when we should be watching the streets, scanning the sky.

Hamid and Rafe walked over to the bride, who was hunched over, sobbing. She sat on the steps of her father's house in her bespattered wedding dress, which was no longer white. Rafe and Hamid both placed hands on her shoulders. Consoling the inconsolable.

There, in the slow relief of the setting sun, the bride's dress turned orange then red. They stood there like that for the longest time, heads bowed as if in prayer.

Nobody said anything.

Everyone had run out of words.

26

Drew

Drew keeps his flaw tucked away, folded and stained, under the webbing of his Kevlar helmet. It is a photo of a woman not his wife. She is turned toward the camera, a smile starting but not yet all the way there. She wears sunglasses that darken her face, but if you could see behind them, you'd find green eyes that also have the tease of joy. Joy is about to break full across her face. She is seeing the ocean for the first time. The wind has taken her black hair and thrown it around her like scarves. Strands are caught in the hinge of her sunglasses, stuck in the corner of her mouth. Drew often untucks and unfolds this photo in order to remember the time three years ago when he and this girl who is not his wife stood on a cliff overlooking the sea at Bandon, Oregon, the wind twisting her hair into knots, her hair flipping his heart into knots. Her name was Tessa and at that moment he was—even as his wife Jacy was at home four hundred miles away nursing their newborn son—falling in love with her. Was *already* in love with her, had *been* in love with her for years—since high school. They'd dated briefly and passionately and he carried her in his heart after they went their diverging ways—Tessa to Bryn Mawr and Drew to the Army—and did their separate things. Tessa got a degree in poli-sci and Drew got married to another girl, Jacy, who he truly did love, cleaving his heart in half and finding he had enough love left over for both women, neither of whom knew the other existed. Alex Drew married Jacy Ramirez in a ceremony bursting with chiffon and lace, tacos made with pork slow simmered in adobo sauce, a polka band, and flower girls dancing ring-around-the-rosy and singing like a record with a scratch and skip, always collapsing in giggles. Alex took Jacy to bed that night never once thinking of his high school flame, putting all his thought and desire and fervor into Jacy's face, her shoulders, her breasts, her generous, embracing thighs. And so it went for three years—"Alex and Jacy, For-*evah*!" he wrote on one Hallmark card—until the night he stayed up after she went to bed and there in a room glowing with light from his computer screen, he received and accepted a Facebook friend request from Tessa Dunlap of Harrisburg, Pennsylvania. Drew was surprised—but pleased!—to see she'd retained the same last name, never marrying in the six years since he'd last seen her. Tessa was interning for a Republican senator from Pennsylvania and, weakened by a fit of nostalgia, she'd decided to reach out to some of her best friends from high school, Alex being the third she'd found. *Hey, remember Cathy Hunderman and Marina Swift? They're still stuck in Nebraska. They never left—can u believe it?!!* And how the heck was he, anyway? Glancing over his shoulder and ready to minimize the window on his screen should he hear his wife's footfall in the hallway, Drew had written back to Tessa with a string of lies and half-truths, never once mentioning his marriage, the son that was soon to come from his wife's womb, or even the fact that he was an infantry scout in the US Army (lies easy to maintain since he never posted anything personal on his Facebook wall, had hardly used it until this moment—no photos of Jacy, their wedding, her ripened belly). He did mention he was living in Seattle—a truth since he was then stationed at Fort Lewis—and he still thought of her often and fondly. Tessa had not written back right away—it was 2:00 a.m. her time and she'd gone to bed after messaging Drew, though he didn't know this. He waited at the computer screen, staring at his near-empty Facebook page and second-guessing that word "fondly" (was he *insane*?). His heart pounded so hard he got dizzy. When he heard his wife waddle down the hall to pee, her pregnant weight creaking the floorboards, he slammed shut the laptop and leapt from his chair as if electrocuted. He gave Jacy a tender backrub that night and though as she drifted back to sleep she wondered why he was doing this right now, it felt so good she didn't question it. The next morning, Drew was up a half hour earlier than usual so he could check his Facebook messages before dressing for zero dark early PT with his unit. There it was: *Hey Alex, so good to hear from you! Seattle, eh? I always wanted to visit there—in fact, have wanted to see the West Coast, which I've heard is the Best Coast, is that true? Can you believe I've never actually seen the ocean—either one? I guess you can take the girl out of Nebraska but you can't take Nebraska out of the girl. LOL!* And on she went for couple of paragraphs of classmate catch-ups. Never any mention of his word "fondly."

That morning during the four-mile run, Drew's heart beat a double-time pace. That night—again staying up late with a lame-ass excuse—he'd written back. She'd written back and he'd answered her again.

One thing led to another and eventually there was this: a plane ticket to Seattle, a lie to Jacy about a training exercise he couldn't get out of, a temporary stash of his packed rucksack in the company storage room, a change into civilian clothes, a drive to Sea-Tac airport, a nervous shuffling from foot to foot at the bottom of the escalators, and a quick hug between reuniting high school friends.

Drew's cell phone started ringing while they were at baggage claim. He ignored it. And then came subsequent rings followed by the vibration of multiple voice mails from Jacy telling him it was *here* and the baby was coming *now* and where was he goddammit, why didn't he answer. Drew put the phone back in his pocket, smiling at Tessa through his worry.

A few minutes later, he got a tearful voice mail from Jacy saying she was sorry for sounding like a bitch in her last message and she realized he was probably in a place out in the field without cell coverage and she'd have her mom get a message to him through his unit.

Drew excused himself for a moment, leaving Tessa at baggage claim while he went to a place away from the speakers announcing flights boarding at various gates. He made a frantic call to his mother-in-law, convincing her not to call his company (she hadn't yet, thank Christ). He told her he was doing everything to get back out of the field and he'd be there as soon as he could, just hold on. When he asked to speak to Jacy, his mother-in-law said it was too late: she was already in Labor and Delivery.

Then Drew sank to his lowest point as a husband: he returned to baggage claim, and when Tessa asked "Who was that?" he gave a dismissive wave of the hand and said "Work," followed by "It can wait," followed by an equally lousy "This weekend belongs to us."

He rolled her suitcase out to his car, and they escaped from the city and drove along the interstate into Oregon with both of them chattering about their lives since leaving good old Hartington High (Drew's half of the conversation almost entirely woven with fabrications).

There came another buzz of a voice mail on his phone. He ignored it.

Then they turned westward off the interstate south of Roseburg and, ninety minutes later, Tessa's eyes widened as the ocean came into view.

They stood on the cliffs at Bandon watching sea lions dive into waves crashing against Face Rock. There was another angry voice mail buzz. Tessa asked: "Aren't you going to answer that?" Drew shook his head, said "Later," and finally, mercifully, he shut off his phone.

Drew and Tessa descended the wooden steps to the beach, walked along the edge of the tide, found a cave hidden from public view, and had a quick, glorious, sandy fuck.

The rest of the platoon thinks Drew's old lady is a smoking-hot babe and that by all outward appearances they're happy. They don't see the times Drew finds a solitary place away from the rest of them so he can reach into his helmet and pull out a photo of a wind-whipped girl not his wife.

If he ever makes it back home, he thinks maybe he'll give her a call and they can talk about oceans.

27

Walking Through the Garden of Eden

"Hey. Hey, Arrow."
"What?"
"Hold up a sec."
"Why?"
"I need to ask you something."
"So ask while we walk. Then fall back in line."
"Okay, but can you just hold up a sec?"
"Keep walking, Fish."
"Fine. *Jesus*."
We keep walking.
"What'd you want?"
"Huh?"
"What did you want to ask me?"
"Oh. You got a cigarette I could borrow?"
"No, I don't got a cigarette you can *borrow*."
"Okay, then."

"If I had a cigarette, I'd *give* it to you, but I wouldn't *loan* it to you. No way I'd want it back after it's been in your nasty cock-sucking mouth."

"Okay, then, can I *have* a cigarette?"

"No."

"What the fuck? You just said—"

"I said *if* I had one. I'm fresh out. You should pay more attention to words, Fish."

"Fuck you, Arrow."

"Sticks and stones."

We walk.

"Helluva country, isn't it?"

"Whatever you say, Fish."

"You think you'd ever want to live here?"

"*Fuck* no. Are you out of your mind?"

"I hear this is the land of opportunity. A guy could get rich here. All that oil."

"Who'd you hear that from?"

"Lots of people."

"Like who?"

"Hoover, for one."

"The chaplain's assistant?"

"Hoover says the Garden of Eden used to be around here somewhere."

"Yeah, well God kicked Adam and Eve out for a reason."

"Hoover says he might move back here after everything's over."

"To look for the Garden of Eden?"

"No, to get rich. Lots of oil, he says. Lots of opportunity."

"Let me ask you something, Fish."

"What?"

"When you were on God's assembly line, did he open up your skull and take a shit in there?"

"Fuck you, Arrow! Fuck you and your mother's nasty twat where you came from!"

"Sticks and stones, Fish. Sticks and stones."

We walk in silence until the wind brings us something bad.

"Jesus, you smell that?"

"Just you and your nasty-ass breath, Fish."

"Smells like something died."

"This whole country is nothing but death. I don't know where you and Hoover get off calling it the land of opportunity."

"I'm just repeating what I heard."

"It was death before we came, it's death now, and it'll keep on dying after we leave. That's the kind of stink you never get rid of."

"Okay, Arrow, okay. Jesus. But I meant more like right now. You can't smell that nasty stank right now?"

Arrow sniffed.

"Smells like more of the same to me."

"Whatever."

"Look around you, Fish. Look at that field over there."

"What about it?"

"You know how many bodies are buried in shallow graves over there?"

"No, and neither do you."

"Not for certain, but if I had to guess, I'd say it was somewhere between a family of five and enough to fill Shea Stadium."

"Funny."

"You see me laughing, Fish?"

"No, but somebody's gonna have the last laugh here."

"The Sunnis."

"Yeah, the fucking Sunnis."

We walk.

"Hey, Arrow."

"What?"

"I didn't mean that about your mother."

"I know, Fish."

"I don't even know her."

"Neither do I. Not really."

"Parents. Fuck 'em."

"Yeah . . . You need to fall back, Fish. Keep your distance. We don't want to give Joe Sunni an easy target."

"Yeah, he needs all the help he can get these days."

"Fall back, Fish. That's an order."

"Okay, okay. But—"

"But what?"

"You sure you don't got a cigarette? You aren't holding out on me, are you?"

"Fall back, Fish."

28

The Secret Life of Men

Arrow is a recovering porn addict. Correction: not recovering, because you never fully leave it behind, do you? All those tits and clits and airbrushed asses remain in your head in some gigantic filing system waiting for you to open a drawer and pluck out the memory of a tilted-back head, a tinny moan coming through the computer, a nipple puckering, a cock being introduced to a glistening bush. It's all still there, *right there*, beneath the soft pad of your fingertip and a mouse click, and you can have it anytime you want. Those unreal, surreal, hyper-real women, their bodies shaved smooth and gleaming like wet seals . . .

So recovering, no. Still wrestling, more like it.

Has he weakened lately? Has he surrendered to the temptation to watch, for the thirty-second time, old favorites like *Star Whores* or *Nightsticks* (that classic 1983 XXX comedy set in a police academy) or even *Every Tom's Hairy Dick?*

Fuck, yes! Yes to the fuck! *Bring on the tits and clits!* he screams quietly inside his sweaty, wrestle-weary soul.

Back in the States, he had his routines. They involved a neatly-folded towel, a dab of petroleum jelly, and a locked barracks-room door. Start to finish, he could get the job done in ten minutes. He had it down to a science. The chemistry of pleasure.

Surprisingly, even on this deployment strictly forbidding anything that would upset host-nation sensitivities—where even a Victoria's Secret catalog is contraband confiscated out of a soldier's duffel bag—Arrow has managed to find a little dick-massage time with an *Asian Yoga Massage* DVD he bought from a street vendor. Just mention "downward dog" to him these days and he gets this weird look on his face.

Tits and clits are not the only things he browses on the web. Lately, Arrow's also been into cock. Abnormally long, hard missiles and swords that wave at the camera, urging him to come closer, take a look, maybe take a bite. He can't understand why, but he can't stop looking at cocks. If Arrow were ever to weaken, let his guard down one drunk night, and let slip a contraband-vodka confession to others in the platoon about this, they'd be shocked but probably not scornful. Different strokes for different folks. So to speak. But if the others were to find out about it on their own—a computer left unattended, a RocketTube visit left undeleted from the web history—and if they confronted him with it, and if Arrow were to protest with a quick self-defense of "I'm straight as the rest of you fuckwads goddammit" and superfluously remind them he was a legend for banging the entire cheerleading squad at his high school in alphabetical order starting with Amber and ending with Willow's pillowy tits in his mouth, well then he'd be in for it. The platoon would show him no mercy.

In his darkest moments of shame—and, as any addict will tell you, the pleasure is always counterbalanced with shame—Arrow has tried everything to discourage himself. He wrapped a rubber band around his penis (not *too* tight, lest it backfire and lend itself to pleasure) and reached inside his boxers to snap it—*hard!*—when the tits and clits (and cocks) grew too vividly tempting in his mind. He chewed tinfoil, he ate whole bags of Cheetos in one sitting, he went for long purging runs that climaxed with hands on knees and a gagging puke—anything, anything to clear his head of t&c (&c).

Arrow has compartmentalized his secret life here in the desert. No one seems to notice he takes his showers alone. No one knows about the rubber band in his pants. And his grief for Sergeant Morgan? It appears to be just like the rest of ours, nothing more and nothing less.

29

The Part Where Things Start to Blur

Looking back, it's hard to sort the pieces in the proper order. There's the pregnant woman—whose pear-shaped face we'll never forget—and the van full of flowers. But before that, there's the house and the bomb makers and the goat tied to a stake. We always get confused.

When telling the story these days, we always put the pregnant woman before the terrorists.

But we're wrong. The bomb makers came first.

30

Who Are You?

We look at Iraqis and think: *Who are you?*

We have come here to this hot hell of a land, leaving our wives and our girlfriends and our parents and our cars and our weight benches, and for what? To protect and bolster a people we don't know, who remain unknowable, who we couldn't give two flying fucks for? And don't even get us started on all that Muslim crap, the medieval bullshit that demands you keep your hot chicks hidden behind black curtains and makes you go all ape shit if one of us happens to sit down in your house, crosses his leg, and points the sole of his shoe in your direction. That shit baffles us.

Some of us—like Sergeant Morgan—have made attempts, have reached across the deep brown chasm to probe and explore and empathize. But look what it got him, Rafe, the ambassador of peace, love, and understanding. It got him blown up. Fucking hajjis bit the hand that only wanted to shake theirs.

We've tried, but we don't know "the people." When we get back to the States—*if* we get back to the States—you figure we'll think about these Ali Babas anymore? Hell no! They'll be even more distant and fuzzy, inscrutable as eroded Sphinx faces, as bland as newsprint.

The only Local National we've come close to knowing in our time over here is Hamid, and even *he* wasn't 100 percent hajji with his Old Navy T-shirts and obsession with Big Macs and *Dancing with the Stars.*

And so, in the middle of our cross-city hike, when we're stopped by the dude we later call Rat Face, we're curious and a little scared. Okay, a *lot* scared.

We're on the dark side of the street, the sidewalk lanced with shadows. We thread our way through too many people, trying to act like we belong here. We step carefully, hearts banging against our armored vests. Somewhere to the north, another dog barks. Then it takes up a howl that sounds like either a laugh or a sob.

We're in bounding overwatch—a classic infantry maneuver—leapfrogging our way down the street: last man rushing ahead, scanning 180 through the sights of his rifle, then when all's clear, the last man jogging up and doing the same. And on and on like that for nearly six blocks.

We imagine we look pretty stupid to everyone else on the street, but this is how we've been trained to move. We are professionals, cogs in the machine, coolly executing the mission. Yeah, right. Most of us, our balls have long since climbed out of our shriveled nut sacks.

All is going fine, we're in rhythm, until Cheever decides now might be the best time for a piss.

For him, it's no longer a question, it's a no-alternative demand made by his bladder, which is doing its muscular best to hold back the flood. Soon, the urethral dam will weaken, break, and flood the terrified residents living downstream in his pants.

He must stop, the rest of us be damned. The piss-urge is so strong it's even overridden the blister pain.

We're moving on, but Cheever pulls up short in an alley striped with shadow and sunlight. The sidewalk crowds have thinned, so he thinks it's okay to take a pit stop. A piss stop. He leans up close to the brick wall, unbuttons, and releases. A dark delta forms a new shadow on the wall and soon there's a puddle growing between his boots. He adjusts, spreads his legs.

The rest of us have moved on without realizing he's lagged behind—until it's his turn to be last man up. O turns, irritated, to say something to him, but he's not there. That's when we hear him cry out. It comes from the mouth of a dark alley a block behind us.

Fish goes, "What the fuck?"

At the same time O says, "That's Cheever."

Drew rushes up and taps Arrow on the shoulder. "Hold up, something's wrong."

Arrow snaps around. "What?!"

"We've lost Cheever."

"Shit." Without another word, Arrow about-faces us and we hustle back.

A man stands at the mouth of the alley, blocking Cheever's exit. He's thin as a blade, but somehow he fills the entire space. Cheever, face white and floating in the darkness of the alley, is still standing there with his cock in his hand, exposed to God, and to the world.

As one, we snap our rifles to our shoulders. We won't fire, for fear of hitting Cheever, but this hajji fuckwad doesn't have to know that.

Arrow shouts something in Arabic, which we assume means something like: "Put your hands in the air and turn around slowly, asshole."

The thin man turns, but doesn't raise his arms. His face comes together in a pinch, like a rat's. All nose and teeth and beady eyes. He's just missing the whiskers.

The man smiles.

There is a black object in his hands. It glints in the sun.

The fact that this guy is not lying in a ditch perforated with M4 holes right now is only because:

a) we're so surprised we're paralyzed,

b) we don't want to draw attention to ourselves with gunfire,

c) if we shoot, we might hit the detonator and it'd be all over for all of us, and

d) one or two of us might have accidentally left their selector switch on SAFE (but we're not saying who).

We scuttle back, trying to distance ourselves from the blast zone. There comes a blizzard of curses. Then we get ourselves squared away and we're all business.

"Down! Down!"

"Set it down, sir, and step away."

"Hands up! Hands up where we can see them!"

The man steps forward into the sunlight and says, "Okay, okay, America. Be cool, be cool." His English is crisp and startling, even better than Hamid's. "I'm putting it on the ground, see? There. There it is." He steps back.

Everyone else who was on the street a minute ago has disappeared. These hajjis are getting smarter by the day. They know when bad shit is about to go down. They know how to ghost-melt themselves right out of a scene.

We get a good look at the man. He's wearing a pair of khaki slacks, thin and shiny at the knees, and a shirt covered with a map of stains and smudges. The clothes hang loose on him and ripple in the breeze, even though there isn't a breath of wind on the street. His tiny eyes move back and forth among the five of us fanned out in front of him on the street. "We're cool, right?"

"No," Drew says. "We are not the fuck cool at all."

Arrow shouts more Arabic phrases at him, but Rat Face just smiles. "No need, dude. English is good with me. But yes," he says to our rifle barrels. "I am getting down. Okay? Okay, okay?" He flattens against the pavement and we're all like: *What the hell is going on here?*

Cheever emerges from the alley, and, with a cartoon tip-toe, steps cautiously around the man and the box he's set on the ground. All the time Cheever's saying, "Sorry, sorry, sorry. I couldn't hold it any longer. I was just going to be a second, and then this guy showed up."

Arrow looks from his rifle sight to Cheever's crotch, then quickly away again, like his eyes got singed. "For God's sake, Cheeve."

Cheever glances down. "Oh, shit." He tucks himself back in.

"Now what?" Drew says. "Arrow, what's our next move?"

Park, the quiet one, speaks up. "I don't like this." He alone, out of the whole group, is turned away from the man spread-eagled on the ground and is swiveling 180s, pulling security for the rest of us dickheads who are standing around with our thumbs up our asses. Park thinks this might be some kind of trap. "None of this feels right," he says.

"I'm with Park on this one," Drew says. "We need to walk away from this."

"Are you fucking kidding me?" Fish's voice is a screech. "This guy comes at us with an IED and we just beat feet?"

The man, flat on the ground, says nothing—but we get the feeling he's smiling into the dirt.

"I'm no bomb expert," O says. "But I don't think that's an IED."

"Sure looks like one to me," Fish says.

"Besides," Cheever chimes in, "wouldn't he have come at us wearing a suicide vest? If that's what he was gonna do, shouldn't we all be dead by now? Me, especially."

"Shut up, Cheever!" three of us yell at the same time.

"I'm just trying to be smart about this," Cheever grumbles.

Fish lowers his weapon and walks over to Cheever and gets up in his face. "Smart? Smart is remembering to grab the PRC-119 out of the Humvee. Smart is packing moleskin in your ammo pouch so you don't have to fuck your buddy over. Smart is thinking maybe it'd be a good idea to tell the rest of us you were stopping to take a goddamn whiz."

O goes, "Fish—"

"I really had to go. It was only gonna be a second, and then this guy—"

"Shut up! Everyone shut the fuck up!" Arrow's voice, high and trembly, stops our voices in our throats. "Give me a minute to think this through. Just one goddamn minute, okay?"

He walks away from us a short distance. He pulls a pack of cigarettes from his vest pocket, lights one, and puts the rest back.

"I *knew* it," Fish says.

Arrow stands there, back to us, his head clouded in smoke.

Half of us watch him, the rest stare at the man in the dirt at our feet, wondering who he is.

Arrow finishes his smoke, stubs it out on the front of his flak vest, then returns to us. He crouches next to the rodent-faced man. He leans down and says something—whether it's English or Arabic, we can't tell.

Rat Face lifts his head. His smile is gone.

"No," he says. "You have it wrong. That is not what this is about. Besides, like he said"—he points at Cheever—"if I wanted to kill you, the police would already be here. They'd be putting you in bags. Little bags. You get me?"

"Yeah." Arrow puts out a hand and helps the man to his feet. "I get you."

"Arrow, what the fuck?!" Fish moves in, but O puts a hand on his chest to stop him. Fish looks down at the hand like it's a bayonet.

"I think we need to trust him," O says. "Arrow's in charge."

Fish has a couple of options here. He can sweep O's hand off his chest and yell, "Fuck you, Olijandro!" Or he could, as Sergeant Morgan was fond of saying, go along to get along. He chooses the latter because, frankly, we all love Specialist Olijandro.

Only Park, still swiveling security, doesn't like this. He shakes his head, doesn't say anything. For now, he'll go along to get along, too.

Arrow has pulled Rat Face to his feet, but he keeps a wary distance. We all do. We don't trust that box of his. There's a good chance we're the dumbest motherfuckers on the face of the planet right now.

"Okay," Arrow says. "Talk."

Rat Face smiles again and it chills us.

31

Objective

Fifteen minutes later, we're walking across Baghdad again—but this time, we are seven.

We're no longer in bounding overwatch, no longer slipping from shadow to shadow. We walk single file like ducklings behind a man in khakis and a stained shirt, a tour guide who's carrying a piece of a bomb, a rat-faced hajji who'll do one of two things: take us to his cousin's house or lead us into an ambush. Our money's on the latter.

All except Arrow. He says he trusts this guy, says he has a good feeling about this, assures us this will be a peek-and-go and then we'll be on our way to FOB Saro. He says, "This is what Rafe would do if he was here." And that, more than anything else, convinces us to go with Arrow's plan.

"We need to get a fix on the bomb factory's location so we can report it to higher," Arrow tells us.

Which is a stupid thing to say because if we have no idea where we are right now, how the hell are we gonna be able to point it out on a map when we get back to the base?

But because it's getting late and we're hot and thirsty and tired, we let Arrow have his way. We go along to get along. We just hope Rat Face was telling the truth a few minutes ago when he got up from his spread-eagle hug of the street.

"I know about the bombs," he said to Arrow.

"Don't we all, motherfucker?" Fish muttered.

The look on Arrow's face, the way he leaned in closer to this twitchy-mouthed hajji told us all one thing: this was quickly falling into a vat of boiling, bubbling bad-luck shit.

"Bombs? What bombs?"

Arrow, Arrow, what are you doing, Arrow?

"I know where they are being made."

"You have credible information you can give us?"

Stop, Arrow. Just stop.

"You are the leader here?"

"That's right, yes."

We look at each other. Mr. Large and in Charge, the Head Cheddar, King Big Balls of Baghdad.

"I know things," the man said. "My information is good. But I think you'll need more men, bigger guns."

"For what?" Arrow tried to read the man's face, to find the lie twitching through the tic of an eye, the down pull of a lip. But, like Olijandro, he thought he saw more desperation than deception. And if there *was* a weapons cache out there, well, that would be worth investigating, wouldn't it? At least report it later to brigade HQ with a best-guess grid coordinate. After we make it to the memorial service, of course—*if* we make it to the memorial service.

"Arrow, what the fuck?" Fish was impatient. "Why are we still standing here talking to this asshole?"

"Yeah, let's go, man." Drew also had itchy feet. "Officially, we're not here, remember? Ghost patrol. We see nothing, we hear nothing, we just glide on past. We're in deep enough, man."

Arrow wasn't listening. "What do you know?" he asked Rat Face.

"These men came into my neighborhood last week. They pushed into my cousin's house. They hit him on head and slapped his wife. It's no good, no good. They're bad, bad men."

"Yeah, and so?"

"My cousin told me they're making bombs in his living room."

"He's full of shit, Arrow. C'mon, let's get out of here. Continue mission."

Now O stepped in. "Did you report this to the IPs?"

"The police?" Rat Face spat. "They're in on it. Their heads are full of blind eyes. My cousin doesn't want any trouble. He told me to stay hush-hush. He said to think of his wife and son—he's got a young boy. Good boy, too. He'll work for the Ministry of Interior someday, that boy. Maybe he'll be police himself. My cousin wants no trouble. He has enough trouble already—big debts and now his wife is pregnant again. Their next child is ready to come any day now. My cousin is a man of worry, always has been. He says to me: 'Never mind, forget it, inshallah, go in peace, cousin.' But I think he's wrong to hide these bad men. I think these men have to go. They're bad for my cousin, bad for his wife and son and the almost child, bad for the neighborhood, bad for Iraq." Rat Face looked at us, sweeping his eyes in a half circle. "When I saw you three blocks back, I thought you could help. So I followed you."

"And you just happened to have a piece of a bomb with you?" Fish said.

"This?" Rat Face laughed. "This is something I pulled out of a trash can to get your attention." He tossed the box away. It fell to the sidewalk with a metal chuckle. "But when I say I want these men out of our neighborhood, I have all the sincerity in my heart. Allah strike me dead if I lie to you."

Rat Face's eyes glittered with what might be tears. This dude was sincere—he wanted these al-Qaeda or mujahedeen or whoever they were taken care of. Eliminated. Tossed in Abu Ghraib and clapped in leg irons. A line from *Star Wars* ran through Arrow's mind: *Help me, Obi-Wan Kenobi . . . You're my only hope.*

Arrow took a shaky breath. He had two options here: he could follow the man back to this supposed cousin's house, leading his squad into the almost-certain death of an ambush, or he could follow this man back to his cousin's house, find a really big motherfucking weapons cache, and become a hero for two days around brigade headquarters.

Arrow licked the dust off his lips, and chose door number two.

He picked up the metal box, looked it over, then smiled and handed it back to the man.

"Looks like this is a piece of credible evidence. We should hang on to it."

And so, ten minutes later, we're walking across Baghdad, a fourteen-legged beetle now. We're less sure of ourselves—and even less certain we'll make it to the memorial service on time. The plan has gone to hell. And all because Cheever stopped to take a piss in an alley.

We do a duckling waddle behind Rat Face. We're going along to get along.

As we walk, our new friend pulls a scarf over the lower half of his face and keeps his eyes downcast when we pass knots of men on the sidewalks. The other men stare at Arrow and the veiled Iraqi, interrupting their conversations until the Americans have passed. Rat Face doesn't speak again until we get near his cousin's house, about five blocks from the edge of the business district.

We stop on the corner, crouch out of sight, and assess the situation. We're across the street from a house isolated at the rear of a dusty yard. To one side of the house, there's a rusted barrel used to burn garbage. A stream of smoke rises from the top of the barrel. Last night's trash. To the rear of the house, there's an abandoned warehouse, its windows blasted out by bombs long ago. Some glass, grayed by dust, remains here and there, like fangs in a decayed mouth. A goat tied to a stake in the yard noses the dirt, searching for a blade of grass. To the right of the house, there's a van with Arabic letters scribbled on the side panels and a big metal sculpture of a daisy bolted to its roof—a flower delivery van, we're guessing. Beyond the van, the ground slopes away to an empty field. A freshly washed sedan is parked along the street, looking completely out of place. To the left, behind a wall, there's another house that was once something magnificent by middle-class Baghdad standards. Not exactly Beverly Hills, but not Detroit, either—some happy middle ground for a family who'd gotten along okay with the Hussein dictatorship. But that was before 2003; now, the entire back of the house is slumped into a rubble of brick and gnarled metal. Bodies, burned and twisted in agony, might still be under there, forgotten in the panic of our blitzkrieg. Birds fly in and out of the broken windows.

Our point is this: if there's a place in Baghdad where you wanted to go build bombs and keep quiet and unseen, this house in front of us is it. It's also an ideal spot for slaughtering a squad of foolhardy US soldiers out here on their own without permission. Easy to make them disappear without a ripple on the war's surface.

Rat Face is, against all expectation, crouched with us. We figured he'd ditch the scene as soon as he got us walking toward the ambush. The fact he's still with us sets our minds at ease. A little.

We look at Arrow, Mr. Man with the Plan. Things have changed now. From the expression on his face, it's pretty obvious this will be no peek-and-go. He means to follow through.

Drew goes, "Goddammit, Arrow."

Arrow shrugs and says nothing. He scans the layout of the yard and the house.

O goes, "Arrow, man. Let's stop and think this through a minute."

"We're here," Arrow says. "We're in the moment. That moment could come and go. These guys could get spooked and hightail it out of here before we can get back to report it."

"So what?" Drew says.

Still in his crouch, Arrow turns to him, gravel crunching beneath his boots as he swivels. "Drew," he says. "Don't you want to do one good thing before we leave this place? Think of all the shit patrols we've been on in the last six months. You really want to go back to the States with nothing to show for this deployment but handing out soccer balls to kids and pulling security at some meet and greets with the sheiks?"

"I just want to get back alive, man. This little sideshow of yours could screw up those odds."

"Goddammit, Arrow," O says.

Arrow is adamant. "We need to do this. And do it quick."

We look at Arrow. We look at Rat Face. We weigh our options.

The house stands quiet and shuttered, the yard empty except for the barrel and the bleating goat tied to a stake nearby.

The day is hurrying along.

Drew sighs. "Fuck it. What's the plan?"

Arrow improvises. We'll give him that. He's tried to mentally map out how this will go and he's planned accordingly. We guess he does the best he can, under the circumstances. But it's still half-assed, even by our company's sloppy standards.

Once we're in place—crouched behind the wall, behind the car, behind the burn barrel—Drew gives the signal, a wink of his mirror, and Arrow nods. He turns to Rat Face. "Okay, here's what I want you to do." He draws a sketch in the dirt between them as he speaks. "Here we are, and here's your cousin's house. I have my men here, here, and here. Okay so far?"

Rat Face nods.

"When I say so, I want you to go up to the front door, knock three times, and try to get your cousin and his family out of the house. Tell them to walk over to this barrel, here, and tell them to get down behind it. That's where they'll be safe. Okay?"

"Okay."

"And then you get your own ass out of the way."

"Okay, sure. I'll try."

"You better do more than try. You only get one chance at this."

"Okay." Rat Face wipes his palms across his pants.

"Now, if it's *not* your cousin who answers the door, if it's insurgents—"

Rat Face frowns.

"The bomb makers," Arrow explains. "If *they* answer the door, then I want you to fall flat on the ground—like this—" Arrow smacks his palms together. "That way we'll know whether or not it's bad guys or your cousin, okay?"

"Okay, sure. Fall down."

"I don't care what you do after that, just get your ass out of the way because me and my men are going in and we're going in fast and ugly."

"Like the movies," says Cheever. He's with Arrow and Rat Face across the street while the rest of the team is positioned around the yard.

"*Not* like the movies," Arrow snaps. "Nothing's ever like the movies."

"Okay, Arrow," Cheever grumbles. "Unwad your panties."

"So"—Arrow looks back at Rat Face—"you got it?"

The man nods and shrugs. That can't be good.

Arrow stares at the Iraqi. "I don't know why I'm trusting you, but I am."

Rat Face puts his hand over his heart. "Truly, I am not shitting you. Believe me when I tell you that house over there is full of bombs."

Across the yard, Drew winks the mirror again, as if to say: *What the fuck's taking so long?*

"Okay," Arrow breathes. "Let's do this." He looks to his left and right. Street's clear. He gives the thumbs-up to Park and Fish. They nod in return, then put their heads back to their rifles, scanning their sectors. "Okay, *go*." He shoves Rat Face out onto the street.

The man composes himself, straightens his stained shirt, then walks across the yard. The goat bleats. It sounds like laughter.

At the door, he knocks three times—not as loud as Arrow would have liked, but loud enough for a voice to come from within. After a minute, the door opens and a man wearing a white dress shirt steps out. Arrow can see what looks like a smeared streak of red running off one shoulder of the shirt. Rat Face raises his left hand and says in a too-loud voice, "As-salaamu alaykum."

The other man returns the greeting, but in a softer voice. He looks back over his red-stained shoulder into the house.

Rat Face takes the man by the arms and talks to him rapidly, urgently.

The goat bleats and tugs its head up and down against the rope binding him to the stake.

The man in the white shirt—we're guessing it's the cousin—shakes his head from side to side, tries to pull out of Rat Face's grasp. Rat Face insists, his voice rising. He looks back across the yard to where Arrow is hidden, pantomiming a cry for help.

An electric ripple passes through us. An alarm clock goes off.

Rat Face and his cousin continue to play tug of war until Rat Face gives a violent yank and tries to drag the other man across the yard. Dust rises in a cloud as they move away from the door and Arrow hears the cousin pleading, "Min fadlak! Min fadlak!"

Please! Please!

Arrow's heart sinks. We're on a speedboat up shit creek. Our element of surprise is blown. Now we'll have to take the place by force. We're kidding ourselves if we think we hadn't been expecting this all along.

Arrow gets to his feet and signals us to start the attack. We rise and are about to move out from our positions.

Just then, another man appears in the doorway. He wears a yellow T-shirt smeared with dirt and grease. He holds a gun in his hand. He calls out in a loud voice and Rat Face and his cousin, halfway across the yard, stop their struggling. Yellow Shirt yells again—this time, a question.

Rat Face lets go of his cousin's arms and, trying to adopt a casual swagger, walks back to the house, greeting the man in a loud, bright voice: "As-salaamu alaykum !"

"Wa alaykumu as-salam," the man returns, but looks puzzled.

Rat Face babbles in a flutter of words, working his hands through the air as he approaches the house. He's laying it on thick. His voice soothes, pats, and assures the man he only wants to show his cousin something in the marketplace or maybe he wants to take him out for dinner and a movie or whatever his excuse is. He might have succeeded, too, if Yellow Shirt hadn't looked up, beyond Rat Face's shoulder, at Arrow and the rest of us caught in the midst of crouching back down behind our cover. We'll admit, not our finest hour. We jumped the gun, so to speak.

It only takes two seconds for the lightbulb to click in Yellow Shirt's head.

He growls, raises his gun, and shoots our new friend full in the face. Rat Face falls back, dead before he hits the ground.

Then he points his gun two inches to the right and shoots the cousin in the chest. The majority of his ribs, heart, and lungs burst through a hole in his back.

Fuck. It's all gone to shit in a blink.

Arrow rushes across the street, stops at the edge of the yard, and takes aim. This stuns Yellow Shirt because he wavers for a regrettable three seconds—trying to choose between firing on the Americans or barricading himself back inside the house. Three seconds is more than Arrow needs.

As Fish later puts it, "The bomb maker's head blowed up good!"

Arrow's M4 chatters a burst of rounds and, behold, Yellow Shirt has a red necklace beneath his chin. There is an eruption, blood shooting everywhere. Something the size of a head bounces off the porch wall. The body, still acting on orders from a brain no longer there, thrashes from side to side, then tries to take a step forward before collapsing in a jelly-legged heap. Yellow Shirt's gun clatters to the porch.

From inside the house come high-pitched shouts from several different voices. Then a scream. Then a gunshot. Then silence.

We move forward in our preplanned swarm of the house. There are two more shots fired at us from inside before we take the objective: one pings off the garbage barrel and ricochets into the side of the goat, killing it instantly; the other—the one, as it turns out, that turns the entire course of events around a new corner—strikes O in his chest, knocking him to the ground. Most of the bullet lodges in the steel blanket of the ballistic vest. *Most* of the bullet. The rest—a shard no bigger than a mosquito—goes elsewhere.

None of us notice because we're fever pitched with adrenaline and moving forward.

Arrow was right. This is what we've come here for. Moments like this are the final exam of all those years of training—from boot camp at our various locations to the field training exercises when we all came together, coalesced into cohesion, at Fort Drum—and going back further, deeper into our selves, when we sat in the movie theater awash with Rambo and Tom Cruise and mud-streaked men straining up a jungled hill with Mel Gibson toward their deaths in *We Were Soldiers*. We were soldiers then, before we became soldiers now. It feels like we have always been soldiers moving along escalators to this moment when we can cock back our legs, boot kick through a door, and shoot bad men—bomb makers—in the chest.

We have not forgotten about Sergeant Morgan and the mission at hand, but he's been moved to the back burner because we're in the here and now and the shit is really real. We are *in the moment*.

In a volley of shouts, rifle clatter, and profanity, Arrow forces his way into the house, followed by Fish, Drew, and Park. They are steel plated. Their legs are springs moving them forward into the uncertainty of the house's interior. Rifles grow out of their faces, sweeping the room, pinning everything down with a metallic stare.

We find seven other men—four of them with soldering irons and circuit boards in their hands, one of the others dropping his AK-47 and raising his hands. He's just seen his friend's head burst in a red mist and he does *not* want to fuck around with these Americans.

As for the other two—well, let's just say they *are* committed and refuse to go down without a fight. They don't let go of their rifles until their bodies have been unstitched with our bullets. We pull our triggers by instinct and reflex and, just like that, we resolve the situation. By the book? No, but we are in the moment and that's all that matters.

That's when the four circuit board hajjis decide they want a piece of the action. They've ducked down beneath their work-table. Seconds later, four AK-47s pop up above the table, care-lessly spraying rounds that embed in the ceiling.

This gives Fish, Drew, and Arrow enough time to bend at the waist, aim their rifles like the well-trained Americans they are, and—*pop-pop-pop-pop!*—take out the trash.

There is an iron-smelling moment as our ears ring with the afterwhine of the shots.

Breathe. Breathe. Breathe.

Our hearts kettle drum. Our eyes sting from the rifle smoke.

A *clatter-slither* comes at us from the corner of the room. We swivel our M4s and find the openmouthed, wide-eyed face of a hajji. The only bomb maker left alive. The smartest one in the room. His arms are in the air. He's kicked his AK-47 across the floor toward us.

Fish sucks in his breath, which sounds like the prelude to something.

"Hold fire! Hold fire!" Arrow yells. "Cease fire, Fish!"

Fish doesn't lower his weapon, but he does exhale like he's finding a rhythm of breath on a rifle range.

"Fish, goddammit!"

With a growl, Fish pulls his cheek off the M4's stock.

Arrow tells Park to secure the AK-47, then zip-tie the pris-oner. That's what Arrow calls him: the prisoner.

Cheever, the chubby coward, finally enters the house, his rifle held at eye level.

"It's over, Cheever," Drew says.

Cheever says, "Okay." He lowers his weapon.

Then Arrow goes, "Park and Drew, you stay with the prisoner. Cheever and Fish, you come with me to search the rest of the house. Clear the rooms and grab any evidence you find. Anything we can carry."

"As *if*," Cheever says. "Like I'm really gonna stuff a pipe bomb in my pack and take it with me to FOB Saro."

Fish, his adrenaline having run its course, goes, "Shut up, Cheever." Then he says, "You stay here and search the bodies. Drew and I'll take this hallway."

"Fuckin' *you* search the bodies." But Fish and Drew have already left the room, joining Arrow as they, one by one, clear the rest of the house. Cheever groans, but walks over to the bodies and gives one of them a feeble nudge with the toe of his boot.

The rest of us go through the rooms quickly, efficiently, like this was a training exercise with NCOs standing by with stopwatches and clipboards.

There's a boy in the bedroom. He's tied to the bedposts—all four of them, so he's spread-eagled for someone's pleasure. He has no pants. He also has a single gunshot wound to the chest. As Arrow stands in the doorway, he watches that hole go *spurt-spurt-spurt*, the blood jets smaller and smaller each time. He turns and leaves after the last one.

Fish finds the mother in the bathtub and calls to Arrow.

The woman crouches in the tub, hands clasped over her head. She says a word in Arabic that's probably something like "don't." She cowers and says, "Don't, don't, don't."

"We won't," Arrow says in Arabic. "Don't worry. We won't."

He and Fish reach forward, take her by the elbows, and lift her out of the tub. She weighs more than they expected. It's only when she's on her feet on the tiled bathroom floor, only when she stands up straight and pulls her elbows out of their hands, they see she's pregnant.

And not just pregnant, but filled-to-bursting-with-baby, any-minute-now pregnant. Now we remember Rat Face saying something about this.

She looks at Fish and Arrow, her eyes going back and forth between them: *Don't don't don't.*

Her face is shaped like a pear and her skin is the color of toasted coconut. If the circumstances were any different, we'd probably think she was a hot chick. Fish, for one, thinks he would do her.

But these aren't those kind of circumstances. Not here in this shot-up house that smells of blood and fear and gunpowder. Right now, she's just another hajji scared shitless by armor-clad Americans.

"You're safe," Arrow tells her. "It's okay, it's okay." He takes the woman by the elbow again and leads her out of the bathroom, through the gore-streaked living room, and into the kitchen at the rear of the house. She walks like a zombie, or the lady from the second row who's been called to the stage by the hypnotist and told to sing "The Star-Spangled Banner" while flapping her arms like a chicken. She can't speak and it's obvious she's not seeing anything except a fog bank in front of her face. Arrow points to a chair and she sits.

Arrow walks up to Fish and says in a low voice, "Keep an eye on her and don't let her go anywhere near the front of the house."

Around that time, Drew comes up and asks if anyone has seen O. Arrow leaves the kitchen calling O's name and we hold our breath, waiting for an answer that never comes. Drew dashes out the front door and finds O on his back near the dead goat.

"O!" Drew cries. Arrow and everyone except Cheever hustle out to the yard. Cheever stays inside with the zip-tied hajji. Because someone needs to stay with the prisoner—and because Cheever is pretty sure he'll puke if he has to see one more dead body.

O is alive. He struggles to sit up, but keeps flopping back.

His mouth opens and closes, wordless, and then the rest of us are pulling off his helmet, patting his legs, loosening his belt, yelling over and over: "Where does it hurt? Where'd they hit you?" O gulps more air, then gasps, "I'm okay! Punched the breath out of me for a moment, that's all." He pants. "Por Dios, it hurts!" He rubs the part of his chest covered by the ballistic plate. "Awww, god*damn*! It stings like a motherfucker."

"Don't be a pussy," Fish says.

"Shut up, Fish," Drew says, still trying to loosen O's belt.

"I'll be fine," O says. "Just feels like I got walloped by a sledgehammer is all."

"Can't say the same for the goat," Arrow says and a couple of us laugh. Then Olijandro goes, "Drew, you fag, would you stop trying to get in my pants?" and we all laugh.

Fish calls out, "Save it for back at the FOB, Drew."

Drew rebounds with: "Whenever you're ready, O, you let me know."

We laugh, getting it out of our system. Arrow says nothing, walks away from the group.

Then it's back to business.

We help O to his feet. He wobbles a bit and breathes like a racehorse at the finish line, but otherwise seems okay.

We have veered off the path. We know this, and we also know we've made a series of mistakes and there's probably some giant cosmic hand somewhere waiting to finger flick our line of dominoes. But you know what? We could give two shits. We've veered, we've fucked up, but the world is also seven bad guys fewer. Soon we'll be back in the States screwing our wives and eating cheeseburgers at the In-N-Out and doing our best to reset our lives back to normal. This afternoon will stick with us for a while, but eventually it'll just be one more thing we did during our time in Iraq.

Eventually. For now, we still need to figure out what to do with the leftover bomb maker. He's unfinished business, which makes him a loose end.

Arrow coughs the gunpowder taste from his mouth. "So, now what?"

We look at him. We thought he had the answers. We were depending on him to map us out of this situation.

"We make it up as we go along," Park says, which at this point turns out to be not just the smartest thing anyone could say, but the *only* thing anyone could say.

32

Land Nav

We've been here before.

      Lost. Confused. Afraid.

Land nav at Fort Drum is no joke. When you are knee-deep in snow and can't see through the fog to the gloves at the end of your arms, when the shouts of others on the course come to you wet, thin, and from all directions at once, when the points you've plotted on the snow-moist map in your hands are nothing but smeared ink and even a six-digit grid coordinate is hard to hold in your head, then you know you are truly good and fucked. There's no laughing in land navigation. There's no crying in baseball.

It's so cold in these woods even the needle on the compass doesn't want to move. Stay still, stay warm. Legs plowing through the snow just stir up the cold and so we slow down—though we know we should be hustling to the next point if we want to make it through this course on time. Nobody wants to recycle through the Warrior Leadership Course and start all over again because of land nav, which right now is totally messing with our heads.

We're sent out in pairs—Arrow and Park, Drew and O—but midway through the course, somewhere around the third point, we come together. We find each other through the trees and snow fog.

"Hey," Arrow says.

"Hey," O answers.

"You guys get anything?"

"We got the first and second points, but we're damned if we can find the next one."

We pull out our damp maps and consult.

"We think our pace count is off," Drew says.

"Even though we both came up with the same thing," O reminds him.

"At this point, we think the cadre are just fucking with us," Drew says.

We look around, as if we expect Staff Sergeant Latham and Sergeant First Class Robertson to jump out from behind a tree and yell: *Boo-yah! You've been punked!*

"We haven't done much better," Park says.

"Shut up, Park," Arrow says.

"What?" Park says. "I don't care if they know or not. We're all in this together."

Arrow and Park have a moment between them, a glance that says: *I told you not to say anything.*

"We'll find the points," Arrow says. "We got this."

"Maybe we should work together from here on out," O says.

"I'm all for that—" Park says, but overlaps Arrow's response. Which is: "Fuck that."

They stab each other with another look.

Park shakes his head, then walks away to find a tree. He fumbles with all the layers of his arctic uniform for a minute, then cocks his head back and sighs as he releases his piss in a steam cloud against the tree. We're guessing he pictures Arrow's face somewhere in the bark of that tree trunk.

Drew pulls out an energy bar, unwraps it, and eats it in four bites.

"Arguing won't get us unfucked," Drew says in a spray of nuts and oats.

"Yeah," O says. "I think we should work together on this."

Arrow pulls out his map and plastic protractor, squinting and wiping snot drips on the back of his glove. He ignores the others and goes right on figuring the six-digit grid coordinate for the hundredth time that morning.

Park returns, saying, "That felt good."

O pulls out a stick of beef jerky. It's frozen and he has to work his teeth on it before the meat tears apart with a fibrous sound.

We sit there, huddled close for warmth. We hear other voices ricochet between the trees, but it's impossible to say where they're coming from. They could be two hundred yards away, or they could be two miles. It feels like the ceiling of fog is getting lower and lower all the time. We don't know if Watertown is ahead of us or somewhere off to the east— wherever east is, anyway. Even the clouds of breath coming from our mouths disorient us. At this point, we'll be lucky if we cross the finish line before dark. We can picture the NCOs with their stopwatches, smirking at us as we stumble to the checkpoint.

Arrow puts his protractor back in his ammo pouch then stands up. "Come on, Park. I think I've got it now."

Park climbs to his feet and cinches his rucksack.

"You're not gonna share?" Drew says. But Park and Arrow are already slipping off through the trees. Park tosses the others an apologetic glance over his shoulder, but he still goes with Arrow.

Drew and O sit there. They can wait for the sun to burn away the heavy weather, but they both know it's no good. The fog of war is here to stay.

"You got any more jerky?" Drew asks. O gives him the last piece, the one he'd been about to pop in his mouth.

Then the two of them stand, tighten their rucks, and head off in the opposite direction of Arrow and Park, purely on principle.

None of us reach the finish line before midnight, our due-back time long past. Once we're all there around the campfire, Latham and Robertson lean back in their lawn chairs and stare at us, standing there bedraggled and shivering. Then they spit snoose juice into their soda cans and tell us to drop and give them fifty.

33

Inventory

COMPUTER CIRCUIT BOARDS (x10)

AK-47 (x16)

M16, AMERICAN ISSUED (x24)

DRAGUNOV SNIPER RIFLE (x3)

RPG (x12)

MILITARY-AGE MALES (7 DECEASED, 1 LIVING)

LOCAL NATIONALS (x2 MALE ADULTS—DECEASED,
   x1 FEMALE ADULT—LIVING, x1 MALE YOUTH—DECEASED)

C4 (x200 LBS)

MORTAR (x1 DOZ)

WIRE, SPOOLS OF (x4)

BALL BEARINGS (EST. 50 LBS)

BATTERIES, 9v (x24)

BATTERIES, CAR (x2)

AUTOMATIC GARAGE-DOOR OPENER (x5)

CELL PHONES, NOKIA (x14)

M67 GRENADE, CRATE OF (x6)

BEANIE BABY (x202)

34

Problem

It all seemed simple and clear, Arrow thinks. Steal a Humvee, go for a drive, pay our respects to Sergeant Morgan, then get back to Taji before too much shit was on the fan. But it had gone wrong almost from the start—spiraling out of whatever control he thought he had. He is ready to say to the hell with it and let someone else take charge of this soup sandwich.

Mostly, Arrow is pissed at how fucked up the situation is. This is on him. The rest of us can offer to share the blame (or, if things go in a different direction, the credit). But in the end, Arrow has to carry this weight. All these dead bodies. Casualties, corpses. He will carry them slung over his shoulders for the rest of his life.

When he walks past Rat Face out in the yard, Arrow takes one look at the shot-away face (he doesn't want to, but it's one of those things you can't not look at) and that brings it down hard and heavy on him. He tells Drew to go inside the house and find some sheets to throw over the bodies in the yard.

The sun is higher and hotter now. We're on full oven roast inside our Kevlars. We hear our brains gurgle to a boil. Some of us drink water; the rest complain about the motherfucking heat. For the thousandth time today.

It's hotter inside the house. Fish says it's all the blood. It's raised the humidity level and that's why we're feeling it in here.

Cheever says if Fish doesn't stop talking about blood, he's gonna yurk up all the chicken he ate. He steps outside, just in case. But one look at the flies hovering like little black helicopters over what used to be Yellow Shirt's head, and he goes ahead and does it anyway. Yurks.

Inside the house, Fish goes through a cardboard box. He holds up a pastel-pink Beanie Baby, a unicorn. There's a knife-slit through its belly. "What do you suppose—?"

"Grenade delivery system," Park says.

"What?"

"Here, kid. Here's a present for you. Go show your mom and dad. They'll be so surprised."

"Oh." Fish looks down at the box. "Shit. There must be two hundred of these things in here."

He looks at the man who's kneeling in the center of the room, wrists zip-tied behind his back. He has his head down and is muttering a bunch of hajji shit over and over. We hear "Allah" a couple of times, but nothing else makes sense.

Fish drops the stuffed animal back in the box. He looks at the man. "You goddamn fuckers," Fish says low, like a growl.

Drew goes, "So now what?"

Arrow feels our eyes on him. He wants to say: *How should I know?* But instead he speaks like he was reading instructions on how to assemble a bookshelf from IKEA: "We move out and we take him with us. For now. Until the opportunity presents itself for us to hand him off."

"Hand him off to who?" Drew says.

"Iraqi, American, I don't give a rat's ass," Arrow answers. "As long as we dump him and continue on with the mission. You know, FOB Saro."

FOB Saro. Shit. In all the excitement, we'd almost forgotten what we were doing out here. Now we think about Sergeant Morgan again. We picture the down-turned M4, the dog tags, and the boots on display at the front of the chapel and we are filled, once again, with rage and sorrow.

"You know what I think we should do?" Park asks.

"Not really," Fish says.

"What?" Arrow says.

"We should leave him here," Park says. "Walk away and be done with this."

"And leave someone else to clean up our mess?"

"Why not?" Park says. "We were never here."

"Ghost patrol." Fish grins.

"You don't think they'll figure out this was no hajji-on-hajji *Godfather* shit?" Arrow says. "You don't think they won't trace it back to coalition forces with the rounds that are in these bodies? Trace it all the way back to us?"

"Worst-case scenario," Park says.

Arrow shakes his head. "Certain-case scenario."

O goes, "Sorry, Arrow. I think I'm with Park on this one." He's still breathing hard and heavy from the blow to his flak vest.

"We need to take him to FOB Saro," Arrow insists.

Leftover Hajji has kept his head bowed. He hasn't looked at us once, nor has he stopped praying.

"I think we should take him out to the front yard and stake him out like a starfish," Fish says. "Let him bake to death. I saw something like that in a Western."

Arrow goes, "You know what, Fish? I've had just about enough—"

"That's a little extreme, man," O says. He's digging in the hole on his flak vest, with his pinkie.

"It worked for Clint Eastwood," Fish says. "Got his attention real quick."

Arrow goes, "Fish, why don't you shut the fuck up, okay? Starting now."

Drew says, "He'll slow us down, you know. Whatever we do, we need to make up our minds and get going."

"Yeah," O says. "Yeah, I'm— We should . . ." He trails off.

"O," Arrow says. "Why don't you sit down for a minute? You're looking kind of pale."

"I'm all right. Like I said, got the stuffing knocked out is all." He looks around at the rest of us. "*Really*. I'm fine, but we should stop shooting the shit and get back on course."

A trickle of blood runs down the small of O's back. It feels like a bead of sweat. O doesn't give it a second thought.

Arrow opens his mouth to say something else, but what we hear instead is a scream. A woman's scream. We turn and look.

The pregnant woman stands in the doorway, swaying. She's slipped past us while we were doing our rock-paper-scissors thing. Maybe she is drawn to the front door by the sound of flies buzzing over Yellow Shirt. Maybe the noise, shock, and confusion are wearing off and she's wondering where her husband is. Whatever the reasons, she's standing in the doorway and she's screaming and screaming without taking a breath. She's seen what's out there—*who's* out there. She stares at the shrouded bodies laid out in the yard. She sees the flowers of blood blooming on the sheets and she screams and screams and screams.

35

In This Way, It Was Decided

Everyone has followed the woman out to the yard.
Everyone except Fish. He's remained inside with Left-over Hajji.

Fish is crouched down in front of the muttering zip-tied man. He stares at the Iraqi as if he were a zoo animal.

Fish has one of the Beanie Babies in his hand. Not the unicorn—a seal.

A seal is slick and sleek. A seal is tapered at one end. A seal can get shoved into a mouth quick as you please.

Fish grabs the back of the bomb maker's head, gets a good grip of hair, then yanks back hard. The mouth falls open, the Beanie Baby goes in. The prayers to Allah stop.

Fish stands up and the man's eyes go wide, then flinch shut as Fish's boot slams into his belly.

After a couple more of these, Fish grabs the back of the man's collar, hauls him to his feet. He has to yank up a couple more times on the collar to get him to stay on his feet. He taps the man on the shoulder then points to the back of the house, to the rubble-strewn yard beyond. The bomb maker goes forward, hunched at the belly. Something in the man's face makes Fish think he knew this was coming, that it was inevitable from the start. That it was only a matter of time until he and Fish were able to have a moment alone to talk things over.

He pushes the man out the back door. Leftover Hajji stumbles over a clutter of bricks, falls flat on his face.

This is not good enough for Fish. He grabs the collar and hauls him to his feet again, pushes him toward the back of the yard.

"Here." Fish stops him. "Right here."

The man goes to his knees without any more shoving from Fish. They both know this conclusion is foregone. Casualties of war, collateral damage, battle tally—whatever words the fobbits in headquarters want to tape over this to make it sound better, easier to swallow. Fish could give two shits. He's doing this and he's doing it now. The rock's rolling downhill. He couldn't hold it back anymore, so he just stepped out of the way and let the boulder crash down the slope.

Like O said, we need to stop shooting the breeze and get on with it. Continue mission.

The Iraqi's back is to Fish. He bows his head. Fish sees his throat working, trying to push more words against the gag. As if a prayer would make any difference at this point.

Fish puts the muzzle of his M4 against the back of the man's head.

Then he realizes he's too close—*don't wanna get no filthy hajji blood spatter on me*—so he readjusts, moves back a few feet.

He raises the rifle. He closes one eye, gets a good sight picture. "This is for the Beanie Babies," he says.

36

Her

"But what about her?" Cheever asks.

We look at the woman. She clutches the corpse to her chest. The sheet has fallen away and now we can see all the damage in the man's chest.

Cheever goes, "Oh, man." He turns away, swallowing another yurk.

The woman's wails rise and fall like a siren.

Arrow goes to her, kneels, takes her shoulders in his hands. He's not trying to pull her away, just letting her know he's there. An attempt at comfort. It's what Sergeant Morgan would have done.

Park goes, "Don't even think about it, Arrow."

Arrow looks up at the four of us surrounding him. He lets go of the woman, stands to face us. "I'm not thinking anything."

"Sure you aren't," Drew says.

"I'm not. Whatever you think I'm thinking, I'm not thinking it."

"Continue mission, man," O says.

"Of course," Arrow says. "Of course. I was trying to show her some sympathy, that's all."

"Right," says Park.

"Sympathy her all you want, but make it quick," Drew says. He's anxious to beat feet, get out of here. He wants to get away from this woman and her belly. Every time he looks at her, he feels the shame of his wife, Jacy, all over again. "Well?" he says. "What now? And don't say 'gimme time to think' again because we have no more time. We're outta time and we need to be outta here."

Arrow *does* need time—and space and solitude. Everyone is crowding him, he can't breathe, he can't get this sorted out.

"Arrow—" O says.

"Shut up shut up shut *up!*" Arrow walks away from them.

Park looks at Drew. O looks at Cheever. Cheever looks at Arrow.

The woman wails and wails and wails.

No one makes a move in her direction. Arrow stands apart from us, hands clasped behind his neck.

The woman has her husband in her arms, his lolling head in the crook of her elbow, and she's rocking him—not to soothe him to sleep, but to wake him from this terrible nap. She calls his name over and over, mixing it with the dying sirens still hiccuping from her throat.

Park goes, "I say we take care of that guy back inside and get the hell out of here."

Drew goes, "Hey, who's watching him anyway?"

Arrow whips around. He says, "Where's Fish?"

That's when the rifle shot cracks from the backyard.

37

No One Said Anything

When Fish was twelve, his uncle got colorectal cancer, stage 3. This gave the man the privilege of going around saying, "Cancer, my ass!"

Uncle Sean was only forty-two, but here he was, shitting away his life in bloody stools. He was hardcore, though. He kept smoking to the end. He'd picked up the habit when he did a few years in Joliet for smashing a biker's skull with an iron bar. Aggravated assault, my ass!

As a boy, Fish always wondered if his uncle had been raped in the showers there, and that's what gave him the cancer. He never dared ask because Uncle Sean flew off the handle whenever someone brought up the subject of what he called fudge packers. He was the kind of guy who'd hit his own nephew over the head with an iron bar if he dared insinuate he'd been fudge packed in a Joliet shower.

God, Fish loved that man with his candy-corn teeth, his eagle-and-flag tattoo spread between the wings of his shoulder blades, his stories of biker gangs and barroom fights, the chicks, the weed, the occasional mini-mart holdup. Uncle Sean was everything Fish wanted to be when he grew up. Untamed. Boundary breaker. Line crosser. A taker not a giver. Rebel yell. The kind of guy who went around cackling at his own joke—"Cancer, my ass!"—even as the joke rotted him from the inside out.

Now as we walk away from our unfortunate detour, Fish thinks of his uncle and smiles. "Baghdad, my ass!" he mutters under his breath, then laughs.

He's the last in line. It may look like we're trying to distance ourselves from him, outwalk him, but this is just the order we fell into as we left the house. Arrow is on point. Fish is rear.

Rear, my ass!

Fish laughs and laughs. No one else says anything.

The sun burns a hole through the tops of our helmets and here's Fish stumbling along laughing, laughing, laughing. Sooner or later, somebody—we guess it'll be Arrow—will turn around and tell him to shut the fuck up, but for now we let him have the laugh.

The last laugh. Joke's on us. We never should have left him alone with Leftover Hajji.

Regrets, we've had a few.

We move along, spring stepping with our legs, trying to work up a breeze, anything to cool our skin. Somewhere behind us, the woman still cups her husband's head in her hand, still screams into the empty air around her house.

O walks slower than usual, breathes heavier. Man, he thinks, the wind really *did* get punched out of his sails back at the house, didn't it?

We don't see O list, or flounder, or start to sink. Not yet, not at that point.

Heat rises from the street. The street is empty. It's us and the heat. Old pals. The bricks under our boots are volcano lava. We walk faster to stir the air against our faces.

We're moving out. *Lef-right-lef-right, hup-hup-hup!* We're leaving it behind us, the whole mess—the bodies of the good and the bad, the wailing widow, the complete fuckaroo we've made of this day.

Nobody says anything. Everybody says nothing.

Except for Cheever, who pipes up with one or two more gripes about his blisters. But that's to be expected. Cheever being Cheever.

Ahead of us, a bird calls out in a rusty voice—once, twice, then it, too, falls silent.

We look up.

38

Rafe in the Belly of the Plane

Sergeant Morgan is moving away from us. "Raphael has left the building," as they say.

We walk across Baghdad—knotted up in the day's gone-wrong events, wondering how to get ourselves untangled—and there's Rafe above us in the transport plane, hurtling through the air at 450 knots, 517 miles per hour. Not a care in the world. Carefree. Footloose and fancy-free. His feet are loose and his fancies are free.

We imagine what it's like up there for Rafe. Maybe he's looking out a window and waving at us.

No, that's not right. He is prone in the belly of a C-17 bound for Dover Air Force Base. Death has made him deaf, dumb, and blind. He can't see us to wave. He doesn't even know we're down here, deep in the shit now, all because of him.

Rafe has escaped Iraq.

This destination of ours? This memorial service? It's nothing but theater, an official government play staged by officers to show: *We really care.* Rafe doesn't care. Rafe could give a flying fuck. Literally.

He's gone, gone, gone. He won't be there at the service to hear all the bullshit nice things said about him—the profane jokes, the comforting words from Psalms, the lies, the half-truths, the flower-strewn eulogies, the script we follow in times like these.

Sergeant Morgan is on his way home right now. Mission complete for him. We're down here sweating in this Baghdad sauna and Rafe is up there in his polished silver casket all cool and composed.

"You mean *de*composed," Cheever says.

Oh, did we say that out loud?

In spite of our sour mood, we laugh and say, "Good one, Cheeve."

We walk on. The heat presses down. The dust rises from our boots.

"Well," Drew says. "At least he's resting in peace."

"You mean 'in pieces.'" Cheever again, the joker.

We laugh. It sticks in our throats, but we laugh.

We picture our sergeant, all twelve parts of him jigsaw puzzled back together again. Overhead lights in the C-17 blink red in the hold's darkness. Rafe's coffin winks on and off, on and off, like a neon sign: OPEN, CLOSED, OPEN, CLOSED. Near the front of the plane, the loadmaster stares at the three coffins strapped to the plane's floor. Correction: not coffins—transfer cases. That's what he's been told to call them. Whatever. He's made sure the transfer cases, the remains delivery systems, the fuckin' coffins, aren't going anywhere. Everything's tight and aligned. Not a wrinkle in the Stars and Stripes. The by-the-regulation alignment of the transfer cases.

The loadmaster yawns.

When he started five months ago, he thought of this as a sacred duty. Back then, it was a solemn, straight-faced, tear-in-the-corner-of-one-eye honor to escort the fallen warrior from battle zone to the black-clad families at the airfield. Now, it's just a job. Sure, he gets to leave Iraq for a little while, but it's not all fun and games. To get stateside, he must first ride with the dead.

Now he's bored, he's tired, he's impatient to reach Maryland, where, as he always does, he'll use his downtime eating blue crabs at Buddy's, looking up a brunette he met two trips ago, and, sitting on a Chesapeake beach, watching the sun rise over the dunes. That's eleven hours from now. He yawns, scratches his anxious balls, then goes back to reading his Louis L'Amour novel.

We're jealous. We wish we had this kind of duty. Shit, we could be loadmasters. Plane rides, brunettes, and crabs. We couldn't fly out of here soon enough.

When the plane banks sharply to the left, Sergeant Morgan's head separates from his neck, the mortician's soft threads tearing without resistance—and rolls off his shoulder to *thump-thump-thump* against the coffin wall.

39

Trail of Blood

As we walk west across Baghdad, going from sunlight to shadow to sunlight to shadow, it becomes obvious to all of us—save one—something is wrong.

There's a disturbance in the Force.

We falter, we slow.

For all our differences, we are the hive mind. We are us against them out here on this mission: us against the heat, us against the street, us against the city, us against whatever will keep us from reaching the service for Sergeant Morgan. We are one team, one body, one fight.

At least, five of us are.

Something is wrong. There's a troubling buzz in the hive. A bad bee.

When we—save one—turn and look behind us, we come to a halt. No fist up, no sinking to one knee, no fingers moving to the trigger housing. We just stop, and stare.

The blood trails away from us in spatter drops, rosebuds on the sidewalk, thicker and heavier where we stand, then thinning to a wispy weave of cat's-paw blots to the east.

We stare at that blood and realize we've miscalculated. A total fucking fuckup. A tire-squealing turn onto Uh-Oh Street. In our haste, we have been fools. All of us—all but one—know we'll pay for our error, our lapse of caution.

O looks at us—his face already ghost white, his eyes already glazed, and says, "What?" He sways like a skyscraper in heavy wind, and says again: "*What?!*"

The trail of blood ends at his boots.

40

Blood Pours Out

Olijandro's eyes dilate. The sidewalk swims in and out of focus. Pain—new and startling—blooms up through his chest. "What?!" He looks at us for an answer we don't have.

"What—what's happening?"

That's all O gets out before he collapses. He goes down hard and quick, his rifle preceding him to the sidewalk in a clatter. He tries to push himself back up, but his arms give out and he slumps.

The sidewalk feels cool to Olijandro and he wants to hug it forever.

Down the street, a boy has been kicking a can back and forth with quick soccer footwork. Now the can clatter has stopped. The boy has seen us. He runs inside—to get help or to hide, we don't know—abandoning the street, leaving us to our work.

We're all over O. We tear at his vest with trembling, sloppy fingers. The Velcro sounds like a curtain torn in half. We loosen straps, pull away the heavy ballistic plates so he can breathe.

This is a big mistake.

Blood pours out like we've tipped a bottle of cranberry juice. It spreads fast, way too fast. We've inadvertently loosened the tourniquet-tight flak vest that's been holding O together for the last hour.

The wound gapes, yawns, stretches for fresh air.

We part O's flak vest, pull away his blouse, untuck his T-shirt. We can see it now, a hole no bigger than a goldfish's mouth, at the base of his rib cage. That dark hole mocks us, throws up a single spurt of blood as if to say: *Peek-a-boo!*

We have no time for questions, no time to be confused, no time to stop and ask: *Didn't he say he was fine? That he just got the wind knocked out of him?*

We rip open his first aid kit, pull out the field dressing, slap it over the wound, our fingers less sloppy now.

"Hold on, hold on, hold on," we chant like it's a hymn and we're in church.

All our training—those cold wet afternoons at Fort Drum, the mannequins with painted wounds, the NCOs with their stopwatches and clipboards—it all surges back to us. We are precise, quick, efficient.

We think again about Savarola and curse him for not being with us right now. We will kick his ass when we see him again.

"Oh, Jesus God," O says in a leak of breath. "O, por Dios . . ."

"Stay with us," we say.

O goes, "Okay, okay, I'm fine. I'm fine." His voice bubbles. "It's just a flesh wound. I've had worse."

Goddamn Olijandro. Monty Python to the end.

Wait. Hold up a goddamn second. *The end?* No way. Not on our watch. This is *not* the end. Not yet, not yet.

Of *course* we think about death. Who doesn't? We're soldiers out here in the zone of death, for chrissakes.

We think about the end all the time.

We eat it for breakfast and shit it out every afternoon.

But this—

We're not going to let it come for us right now. Keep your distance, motherfucking Reaper.

We're gonna hold on, hold on. O, buddy, can you hear us? You stay with us, okay?

We tie the bandage. We rip open our own first aid kits, get another bandage ready. Just in case. We gather fallen palm fronds from the street, we hold them over O to keep him cool, make him comfortable. One or two of us pray, though we're not the praying kind.

O goes, "It's just a scratch." His voice trails off. A red bubble appears at the corner of his mouth, grows, pops.

41

In Delirium

His ex-wife leans over him. "Hey, you all right?" She touches his bandage, but it doesn't hurt. In fact, it tickles. He laughs—a bubbly gurgle—and *that* hurts. Oh, por Dios, it hurts like nothing's ever hurt before, like it was the first pain his body ever felt.

"Stop," he whispers, and she takes her hand away from his ribs.

Melinda brushes her fingers across his forehead, as if to sweep back a lock of hair. "You used to have beautiful hair," she says. "Black as the night. Where'd it go, mi corazón? I miss your hair."

Black as night. Black night. The Black Knight. That movie they loved. *Monty Python and the Holy Grail*. He and Melinda saw that one over and over.

"Remember, Melinda? Remember how we laughed? And sometimes we didn't even know why we were laughing?"

"I remember, O. We remember." Fingers brush across his forehead. "Now, *shhh-shhh-shhh*."

That scene where the Black Knight loses the sword fight with King Arthur and ends up dancing on one leg, tomato-juice blood gushing all around. He taunts Arthur, saying his wounds are merely scratches, but all the time there's this blood spray. He goes, "I've had worse." Blood jetting out of his amputated limb stumps. The Black Knight mocks King Arthur, saying if he didn't stand in one place and fight, he'd bite his legs off. And that was some funny shit. O and Melinda bent over double, slapping their own legs.

Legs. Oh God, his legs are so cold. The chill is rising up his body. Like blue rising up in a thermometer measuring ice. A reverse thermometer.

He's going in reverse. The camera pulls back. He's slipping away.

Not yet, not yet.

"Swim against the tide, O."

"Okay, Melinda."

"Swim to me."

"I'm trying."

Melinda bobs in the waves. She's nothing but a head and shoulders. *Pero que bella es, so beautiful. The prettiest fish in the ocean. Mi corazón.*

"Stay with us, O."

"Okay."

"Swim to me, O. Take my hand. Can you see my hand? Grab my hand."

The waves are strong, but O is stronger. He pushes through; he pushes through as hard as he can. He swims to Melinda. He can't see her hands, but he knows they're there. It's a matter of finding them.

"Take my hand, O."

"Hold on, O."

"Stay with us, O. Don't you dare leave us. You hear us, O? Don't you dare go out on us."

42

Huddle

We stop O's bleeding. It takes a succession of bandages and yards of tape and O's side looks like a Christmas gift wrapped by a four-year-old, but he's stable. He's pale and weak, and barely with us—but at least he's with us, right?

We move him to a shady spot, lay him against the side of an abandoned warehouse. High above our heads is a faded sign painted on the stucco in Arabic that none of us can read, not even Arrow, but there's a cartoon drawing of a tire rolling along a road, flying through midair with horizontal lines streaming behind it. An illusion of speed and forward movement. But that tire's not going anywhere.

We elevate O's feet to prevent shock. He's still with us enough to look up at the warehouse sign and make a joke: "God, I'm so tired."

At least we *think* it's a joke.

Cheever stays with O while the rest of us move away to talk.

The first thing Arrow says is: "I'll carry him."

"The whole way?" Fish says.

"I'll do my best."

Drew goes, "Not in this heat."

Arrow shrugs. "So, we carry in shifts. It's only, what, another couple of klicks to the ECP?"

"By whose count?" Fish says. "We don't know a damn thing."

"We've got to be getting closer," Arrow insists.

None of us mapless fools know for certain, of course, but we doubt the Entry Control Point to FOB Saro is less than two kilometers from our current location. In our heads, that guard shack retreats from us like it's on a conveyor belt. Unlike the tire, it *is* on the move.

"O needs help right now," Arrow says. "Our quick-fix patch isn't gonna hold for long."

"One bad coughing fit," Fish says. "Then he starts gushing all over the place."

"Well, aren't you Suzy Sunshine?" Drew scowls at Fish.

"What we need is a hospital," Arrow says.

"Look around you, man. Not exactly one on every corner here."

This neighborhood is a wasteland. We've been walking through a deserted zone of factories and empty fields ever since we left the bomb makers' hidey-hole. Nothing moves—no cars, no people, no dogs, not even a piece of trash tumbling on the breath of the wind. Because there is no wind in this oven. We're out here on our own. Men against the landscape. Men against the circumstances. Men against the clock.

"We'll never make the memorial service now," Drew says.

"Forget Morgan," Fish says. "Unless we move out right now, we're looking at a double-casket service."

"Wow, that's harsh, dude."

"I calls it as I sees it. The longer we stand around with our dicks in our hands, the harder it gets for O."

"You mean the harder your *dick* gets. Cuz it loves your hand."

Fish gets all up in Drew's face. "Only reason I'm not kicking your ass for that right now is because it's too hot and you're not worth it."

"Fine. I'll take a rain check."

Arrow has had enough of this. "Shut up, both of you!" He looks over at Cheever. He's fanning O's face with a palm frond. "I still say we carry him. And I say we move out. Now."

Fish sighs. "You're the boss, boss."

We break the huddle and move back to O and Cheever. That's when Park, who's been silent this whole time, stops us and says, "Wait. The van."

43

Blow Job

This is all his fault. You trace the lines of everything that happened today, the many branches of paths and options and choices, and it always comes back to him. It's Cheever's fault.

This is what he thinks as he sits beside O, fanning him with a palm branch.

Leaving the map in the Humvee. Slowing them down with his blisters. Stopping to take a piss. All roads lead back to John Hubert Cheever.

Cheever's spiraling down, getting darker by the minute. He's reached his limit, physically and emotionally. He can't do this anymore. He's gotta stop fooling himself, and the others. He thinks, *They'll all be better off if I just go away, follow the whirlpool drain to the end.*

He needs to find somewhere safe, somewhere we can't see him and stop him. Somewhere it'll be just him and the M4.

Cheever doesn't think about us, how we'll feel about his trigger pull. He does think, however, of his mother. Her face when she gets the news, how she will collapse into a sinkhole of grief.

He thinks about the muzzle. He thinks about how it will taste when he lays the tip against his tongue. He thinks about how the metal will click against his teeth. He thinks about his lips closing over the shaft of the barrel.

Cheever has never given a blow job in his life, nor has he ever received one. This will be his first and last fellation.

Actually, the M4 will be the one giving *him* the blow job. He grins. Yep, it'll blow him, all right. Blow the back of his head clean off.

Good one, Cheeve.

At Cheever's feet, O groans, moves his head side to side. He's slipping in and out of consciousness now.

Cheever kneels beside him. "Hey," he says. "Hold on, O. Hold on, dude." He puts a hand on O's shoulder. "You stay. I'll go."

44

Backtrack

"Hey. Hey, Park."

Fish is a few paces behind Park, who's really moving out now, double-timing back the way we came. It's just the two of them, sent back for the van parked beside the bomb-making house.

"Hey, Park. Slow up a minute." Fish is out of breath, but he jogs harder to catch up. "Hey, man, you got a cigarette?"

Park says nothing, keeps marching at quick time. *Hup-hup-hup*. It's Sergeant Morgan saying that: Park hears Rafe calling the cadence in his head. This makes Park go even faster.

"Didjoo hear me, Park?"

Park heard Fish just fine. Fish knows Park doesn't smoke, never owned a pack of cigarettes in his life. So why is he bugging him about it? Why is Fish wasting energy flapping his jaw when he should be stretching out his legs, conserving his breath? Park abhors waste. And Fish is nothing but a waste. He's one of those windup chattering monkeys. His words are toy cymbals bang-bang-banging.

"I could use a smoke right now."

They walk, jog, walk.

"The silent treatment, huh? Jesus, Park, you're something else." This whole mute, enigmatic facade is starting to bug the shit out of Fish. Who does Park think he is? The Buddha of the battalion?

"Must be a Japanese thing," Fish says.

That stops Park.

"Korean." His voice slides out thin as a knife.

That's it. One word, then they're back to hustling down the street.

"Whatever," Fish mutters and jogs to stay with him.

They pass street after street, searching right and left for familiarity, trying to look as normal as any two heavily armed Americans running across Baghdad on a sunny afternoon would be. Just a couple of tourists on a scavenger race through the city.

"What if the keys aren't in the ignition?" Fish says, just to say something. They've already discussed this. No keys, then they hot-wire the van. If that doesn't work, they'll look for another car, motorcycle, rickshaw, whatever they can find to transport O to FOB Saro.

But for now, the van is the thing. This is our new target of opportunity—ever since Park remembered seeing it parked beside the bomb-making house—the delivery van with a cracked windshield and a daisy on top.

"The van" was all he'd said back there. He hadn't needed to say more. The rest of us remembered it then, too. That dusty, rusted vehicle slumped beside the house. It's exactly what we need for O right now. Why hadn't we thought of this sooner?

O.

Jesus. How could we not have seen this coming? How could we have been blind to his stagger, his wobble when we pulled him to his feet? How could we have thought everything was fine when O said not to worry—*just a punch of wind*. How could we not have heard the weakness in his voice? How could we not have known he was saying those things only to keep us going on the mission, even though he knew—he *must* have known—his life was draining away?

"Park's right," Arrow said. "We've got to go back and get the van."

Were there weeds growing out of the grille? Were the tires flat? We couldn't remember, but it didn't matter. We'd drive on metal rims, if that's what it took to get O to the aid station on FOB Saro.

Park and Fish drew the short straws for the mission. Lucky them.

They knew where they needed to end up, but weren't exactly sure how to get there. Before we had to stop for O, we took so many turns, too many lefts and rights.

When Fish and Park started, they could follow O's blood trail. That was fine for about two blocks, but then it wisped away to nothing.

They argued about directions—both had their hunches—until Park, hating himself for doing it, caved in to Fish and they went his way.

Until they came to the Tigris and to a stop so sudden it was like they were in a cartoon, dust boiling around their feet, and they knew they'd fucked up.

We hadn't seen the river at all today.

"Well, shit," Fish said. "Can I get a do-over?"

That's when Park stopped listening to Fish and took point on this mission. They backtracked to a familiar spot and when Fish said he thought they should go right, Park went left, and got them back on course.

Now they hustle, push their way past uncertainty and misdirection.

"You think he'll be okay, Park?"

"Dunno."

"He was looking awfully pale when we left."

"He's bleeding out."

"You don't like him, do you?"

"I never said that."

"Well, you're acting all cold and shit right now, Park."

"I'm focused."

"Okay, Buddha. But can we at least stop and catch our breath?"

They slow to a walk. They're on a paved road and it's baking them from the boots up.

Fish goes, "I get the feeling you didn't even like him."

"Are you kidding? Everybody loves O."

"I meant Morgan. You were never chummy with him or anything."

"He was my platoon sergeant. He wasn't supposed to be my friend."

"That's not how everyone else sees it."

Park takes up a light jog again, breaks away from Fish.

It doesn't work. There's no getting away from Fish and his mouth.

Park looks over and goes, "Why are *you* out here?"

"To pay my respects. What else?"

"Respect? You're the fucking new guy, Fish. You didn't know him."

"I knew him well enough."

"Not like the rest of us."

"I knew him enough to come out here with the rest of you fucktards today, risking life and limb—"

"Save it for the eulogy, Fish."

Park slows to a walk. Now he's out of breath, too. This heat is squeezing him to a faint.

Fish is still nipping his heels. "You didn't answer my question."

"Which was?"

"Did you like Morgan?"

"I liked him well enough," Park says, then clams up.

They keep their heads on a swivel, stay close to buildings, flinch at odd sounds. They sip water through the tubes of their Camelbaks.

"Stay hydrated," Sergeant Morgan tells them. His voice is in their heads. It is loud and unbending.

They drink. The Camelbak water is warm and tastes like the inside of tires. Fish swishes his around, then spits it on the ground.

A dog dashes out from a yard to greet them. It sniffs the spat-out water, then licks the road.

Fish feints toward the dog. "Go on, scat!" For some reason, this dog licking his spit bothers him. He'd probably butt-stroke this dog if Park weren't here.

Dogs bother Fish. They're all slobber and mange and ball licking and leg humping when you're visiting your girlfriend's house for the first time. He had his way, he'd like to see every dog over here in Iraq roasting on a spit. Trying selling *that* in the marketplace. It'd probably be like goddamn caviar to hajji.

Fish makes another lunge toward this back-alley dog now and it scurries away with a yip.

They trot down the road and drink their rubber-flavored water.

"We've gotta be getting closer, right?" Fish says.

"I don't know. Anything looking familiar to you?"

"Not really. You?"

"Maybe. But I don't know."

They tense when they hear the sound of motors. They step off the road. They pull their rifles flat against their chests. Their index fingers find the triggers.

Two cars approach, slow as they draw even with Park and Fish, then accelerate. The soldiers are left in a fog of dust.

"Fuck you very much," Fish mutters.

The last vehicle's brake lights flare—as if the driver heard Fish—but then blink off again and both cars are gone around the corner. It felt like a moment, or something that was about to be a moment, but in the end it was nothing more than two cars passing two men walking along the side of a road. Just another thing on an ordinary day.

Park and Fish unclench their sphincters.

Fish goes, "Shit."

Park goes, "Close one."

They look at each other. Something passes between them—an understanding, maybe. At the very least, an acknowledgment they just shared something.

They start walking again.

Eventually, things look familiar.

"I think we're almost there," Fish says.

"We take a left at the next corner," Park says.

"Yeah, I think you're right."

Park smiles. "Your momma was home when you left—"

"You're *right!*"

"Your girlfriend was home when you left—"

"You're *right!*"

They pick up a rhythm and it feels like old times again. The two of them—no matter how they each feel about Rafe—wish their old platoon sergeant could be here with them, off to the left, barking cadence and making the walk bearable with his sing-song voice.

45

This Ain't No Movie

Back at Olijandro Central, we have the patient stabilized and we're scrubbing up at the sinks, talking about last weekend's golf game.

We like to think we can crack jokes at a time like this. That's how we roll.

The truth is, O seems to be doing better. The bleeding has slowed to a seep and some color is coming back to his face. He keeps asking for water, so that's good, right?

Or maybe we're kidding ourselves, desperate to make sure this day has a happy ending—as happy as things can be over here.

"Hey," O says in a frog croak.

We go up to him, kneel, lean in closer.

"If I don't make it, tell my ex-wife—"

"Naw, none of that, man!" Arrow says. He places his hand tenderly on O's forehead and keeps it there.

"Save that bullshit for the movies," Drew says.

"I'm serious," O says. "If I don't make it, you gotta tell her—"

"Private Olijandro," Arrow says. "We're not listening."

Cheever holds a canteen to O's mouth. "Drink up and shut up."

He takes several gulps, nods at Cheever to stop. "I love you, babe."

Cheever, Arrow, and Drew look at each other.

"That's all I wanted to say to Melinda. Four words. Think you can remember them?"

Arrow moves his hand to O's shoulder. "We'll remember. We'll remember to make sure you tell her yourself, you asshole." Arrow smiles at him. We all smile down at O.

"Hey," he says. His voice is weaker, foggier, and we have to lean in to hear. "You guys have to tell her those were my very last words. Just like in the movies."

We fall silent, not knowing if we should laugh or cry.

"How 'bout them Yankees?" Drew says after a moment.

"Best season ever," Arrow says.

Wind rolls down the street, spirals up a cone of dust on the other side of the road, then passes on, like a tan ghost here and gone.

"How long since they left?" Cheever asks.

Arrow checks his watch. "Thirty-five."

"Feels like three hours."

"Everything's longer when you're waiting."

We fall silent again, scanning our sectors of fire though we seem to be the only ones out here.

Cheever goes, "What if they don't make it back?"

"They'll be back," Arrow says. "That's how this movie is gonna end. They'll be back and everything will be okay. Happy endings for everyone."

"Might I remind you that you yourself said this ain't no movie not too long ago."

46

Wheels

It's all good. None of the tires are flat and there's no bristle of weeds poking from the grille. One of the windows in the back is broken out, but other than that it looks drivable. They've misremembered the condition of the van—to their relief—and, best of all, Fish thinks he can get it going.

When he and Park open the driver's door, the van exhales hot breath that smells of:

Honey.

Lavender.

Earth bloom.

Rose petal.

The van is full of flowers. Heaps and heaps of them: careless bouquets tossed in the back, long overdue for delivery. A bench seat runs the length of the interior, but other than that, it's nothing but flowers, flowers, flowers. The smell is potent, sweet, overpowering.

Fish thinks of his grandmother and the times she'd pack him into a church pew filled with all her old lady friends, each of them in proud ownership of a special bottle of Sunday-go-to-meeting perfume, each of those lady smells colliding and pounding against little Fish's nose.

Park remembers gardens he and his grandfather once visited in Seoul.

If the rest of us had been there with them, we'd have each been overwhelmed by our own memories. One or two of us might have gotten choked up, thinking about the places those flowers took us.

Armed with nothing more than his Leatherman pocket knife, Fish goes to work under the dashboard, sweating and grunting.

Behind Fish and Park, the bodies of the men and the goat fester in the midafternoon heat. Flies still scribble a dance in the air above what used to be Yellow Shirt's head.

Park and Fish keep their backs turned as they work on the van. They can't deal with that shit right now. The yard is quiet except for the fly buzz.

Fish works on the wires, snipping, stripping, striking, sparking. The engine coughs once, twice, then turns over. He crawls out from beneath the dashboard and looks at Park, wiggles his eyebrows.

Park is impressed enough to give him a high-five.

Fish could savor the moment—the engine rumbling, Park almost smiling, the flies briefly startled away from the bloodmess—but there's work to do. They have to get going. Continue mission.

"I'll drive," Fish says.

"I call shotgun."

"Good one, Park."

They pull out of the yard, more than ready to leave the house and its gory yard behind. It feels good to be off their feet, to be rolling on wheels again. Fresh air flows through the broken window and ripples through the flowers.

They've gone two blocks when Park puts a hand on Fish's arm. "Hold up. Did you hear something?"

"Hear what? I didn't hear any—"

But then he hears it, too.

A groan, a whimper, a cry that's about to climb the scale to a scream.

Fish slows the van, pulls to the side of the road. The two of them turn in their seats, look at the back of the van. The mound of flowers is moving, rippling. Something is there, struggling to emerge.

Park and Fish reach for their rifles.

47

Scream

The van screams as it approaches.

Arrow, Cheever, and Drew get to their feet, grip their M4s.

"Is that them?" Cheever asks.

Arrow and Drew have their rifles raised. They aren't ones for stupid questions. That van is coming at the kind of speed for which rules of engagement were written.

"That's our ride, right?" Cheever asks again.

Neither Arrow nor Drew see the metal flower sprouting from the roof.

The van howls, cries, screams again: a primal human sound rising above the *clatter-purr* of the engine.

"Fucking A, fucking A," Drew says as the vehicle comes at us fast. Too fast. It approaches in a cloud of dust, like Pigpen from a *Peanuts* comic strip.

Arrow has seen something. He shouts, "Hold fire! Hold fire!" But Drew's finger is already on the trigger, halfway to commitment. Then, through the haze beyond his front sight post, he makes out Park's face. It's pressed close to the windshield. The glass is coated with dust and Park is out of focus, but now Drew can see it's him, Park, and not some terrorist on the attack. His mouth is rounded in an *o* like he's yelling, "Don't shoot! Don't shoot!"

Drew lowers his rifle. "Is Park screaming?"

"C'mon, *Park?*" Arrow says. "When was the last time you heard anything above a whisper from him?"

"*Some*body's screaming," Cheever says.

"Thanks, Captain Obvious," Drew says.

"Guys—" O says behind them, but in all the noise and confusion of the van pulling up, he goes unheard.

Arrow slides open the side door.

Flowers. Jesus, all those flowers. Enough for ten funerals.

"Whoa!" Drew covers his nose and mouth with the crook of his elbow.

Cheever goes, "It's like a greenhouse farted."

This is no time for jokes.

Park is all up in our faces. "What the fuck, Drew! Were you really just about to pop some rounds at us?"

Drew goes, "Sorry, man. Mistaken identity."

"C'mon, hurry up," Fish says, turning in the driver's seat. "Get O loaded. We need to keep moving."

The van is still screaming.

We peer through the dark jungle inside the van. There, in the back, among dozens of rotted bouquets, a woman writhes like she's at a high school wrestling meet and doing her best not to get pinned to the mat. It's her—the pregnant woman from the bomb makers' hideout. In a mind blink, we understand what's going on—and we don't like it. This wasn't part of the plan. Not even close.

Park snaps, "Get in, get in."

If Park is freaking out, that means this is some serious shit all right. As gently and quickly as we can, we load O into the back of the van beside the woman. His torso is slick with blood. Too much blood.

Cheever gathers the gear and leaps inside. The door slams shut behind him.

Arrow calls out, "We're good, Fish." He makes his way forward and tells Park to get in back. King Big Balls will ride shotgun now.

And then we're off. We're back in action. *Hail, hail, the gang's all here!* This time in a legitimate motor vehicle. *We're back, ba-by!*

Then Cheever is at it again: "Will somebody please tell me what's going on?"

Fish, Arrow, Drew, and Park all say it at the same time: "Shut up, Cheeve!"

The van jerks forward with a gear crunch and heads down the street, bringing FOB Saro closer.

Along the way, Park gives a sitrep. It's more words than any of us have heard him say at one time, all strung together.

48

On the Road Again

With Arrow navigating, we take wrong turns, hit dead-end streets, and are forced to make three-point turnarounds. With every lurch and reverse, the frustration rises. This feels like that land nav course at Fort Drum all over again. We're spinning compasses in a foggy forest.

Arrow clenches his jaw, grits his teeth.

This should have been easy from here on out. The van should have been the solution.

The woman's screams have died to a drip of moans. She rolls her head from side to side on her bed of flowers. Her body is soaked with sweat. Her eyes are closed. Like she's praying.

We're no doctors, but we're guessing the contractions have died down or something. Don't they come in waves?

Drew thinks if he'd been at the hospital with Jacy he might know about these things. He winces as that knife twists, digs deep into his gut.

The stowaay woman huffs like a boiling teakettle, but at least she's stopped screaming for now.

O lies beside her on this floral mattress. His eyes are closed, too.

"How's he doing back there?" Arrow calls over his shoulder.

"Holding steady," we say.

But we're lying. O is slipping, fading, falling away from us. His breath is shallow and he won't open his eyes.

"O," we say quietly, so Arrow can't hear. "O, stay with us, man."

"Hey," he whispers. Or maybe it's "okay." It's hard to hear him because the woman's moans are on the rise again.

Drew goes, "You had to bring her?"

Park says, "Fish wanted to leave her. Said to dump her beside the road."

"Jesus."

"Said she was just another piece of useless baggage."

From the back, we look at Fish. He turns the steering wheel left and right as Arrow guides him through the streets. He looks happy to be doing something useful.

"That's cold—even for Fish," Cheever says. He gets up from the bench seat and kneels beside the woman.

The woman senses the soldier next to her and opens her eyes. She looks right at Cheever—deep into his eyes—and, get this, she smiles. She smiles at Cheever, our suicidal jester who has been the cause of the day's major wrong turns. She smiles at him and it stuns Cheever for a minute, this note of grace. He reaches out and takes her hand. He smiles back. "Hey there," he says.

Up front, Arrow tells Fish: "Take a left at the next corner."

"Are you sure?" Fish says.

"No. But it feels right. Take a left, Fish!"

The van veers and our bodies shift right.

We hear Arrow go, "Yesss!"

We look out through the windshield. "What?"

Arrow points. "There. Doesn't that look like the mosque we used to see from Route Irish when we made our supply runs to Saro?"

We look and, though we can't be sure, we tell Arrow we think it is.

If we can get to Route Irish, we can find FOB Saro.

We're almost there.

49

Flowers

Almost there, almost there.

O is happy. He runs through a meadow hip-high with flowers. Roses everywhere. All colors: white, yellow, lavender, royal blue, and of course blood red. And get this: not a single one has thorns. O slips right through them as he sprints across the beautiful sea of flowers.

His wife—not his ex-wife, his *wife*—stands at the far end of the field. Melinda waves her arm, beckoning him. O bounds forward. She calls to him. She is backlit by a setting sun that's turned the meadow a rich gold. It's beautiful as a movie fade-out.

O thinks, *Everything is going to be good from here on out, mi corazón. We're golden.*

O runs through the roses. His wife is bathed in light, she glows with sunset, and she wants him once again. O runs toward her and he is happy. The happiest he's ever been.

50

Death

Shortly after 9:00 a.m., your platoon enters a neighborhood in eastern Baghdad—the section they're now calling New Baghdad. As if the name, like a fresh coat of paint on a turd, could make a difference.

You are there to establish a checkpoint as part of a secure perimeter—a cordon, in military terms—while another unit from a different American brigade searches for a suspected IED somewhere inside the perimeter. You are the platoon sergeant, the big guy in charge (even though you're not tall and you know to keep your head down—especially around bullying officers and senior NCOs). You go about the business of getting your men in place. You already went over this mission earlier back at Taji, drawing with arrows and squares in the dirt outside the motor pool, so now it's just a matter of setting everything in motion. You love your men and they love you back, so things should go okay.

The day is already hot and heavy at 0900 hours. Along the cordon, your gunners behind their .50 calibers scan their sectors of fire, watching for anything out of place. A flash of light from a second-story window. The wide berth pedestrians give a dog carcass. A man dressed in unseasonably heavy clothes speaking into a cell phone. Anything, anything at all. The gunners have tunnel vision. Their minds buzz like hives. Their eyes zoom and focus like telephoto lenses.

The morning is hot and dusty and unravels slowly. You're told this operation could take a while. You and your men settle in for the long haul.

It's quiet here along the perimeter. Your soldiers mutter to themselves. In the lulls of conversation, the static bursts from their radios are like fuzzy explosions that make them flinch and cower.

Some soldiers, not as alert as the gunners, get out of the Humvees—not only to stretch and smoke, but to greet the children who have rushed the military checkpoint, as they always do when the Americans roll through. You yourself love the children. They remind you of your brother's daughters and sons and oh, how you always loved spending Christmas with them—the laughter, the smell of new toys, the goodwill and peace on earth, if only for a day or two. Now, these Iraqi kids make you feel good, like Christmas was paying you a visit in summer. Right or wrong, you always allow kids like these to break down your military discipline. Your men turn a blind eye.

"Mister! Hey, Mister!" the children shout, their palms out, their fingers splayed. To them, you're a candy machine, a big camo-clad sweetshop. The Americans always carry bags of Jolly Ranchers and chewing gum, drawing kids to them wherever they go. If they're lucky, they'll get a Beanie Baby or a soccer ball.

Today, you and your team give fistfuls of candy to the first wave of children, but then you make sure Arrow and Park and the others turn back to the business of keeping the perimeter secure. The children keep coming with their fingers and cupped palms.

"No more, no more today," your soldiers tell the children. You, on the other hand, still have a secret stash of Jolly Ranchers in a cargo pocket. You'll wait for just the right moment to break it out.

The children keep crowding your checkpoint. Your soldiers hate to do it, but they put on their tough-guy masks, scanning the streets and trying not to look at the little rug rats, hoping they'll get the message and go away. It hurts to ignore the kids, but it has to be done. Mission first.

After half an hour, maybe the children have forgotten about the candy, or maybe they're curious about your gear—the Camelbaks, the flak vests, the flashlights and earplug cases dangling like jewelry. Maybe they practice some giggly high-fives with their American heroes.

The soldiers play along as best they can, keeping one eye on the road and the shadowy houses while bumping knuckles with the kids in a gruff-tender acknowledgment.

The children persist. Now they're laughing and pretending to play grab ass with your soldiers. It's all happy fun. You play along.

In fact, you really get into it. Things are quiet in this sector and it feels permissible to unclench the sphincter. You have a few words with Arrow, the specialist and soon-to-be corporal if you have any say in it. You put Arrow in charge while you take a moment with some of the kids. This is a war zone but a guy's gotta relax every now and then, right?

As you turn back to the children, you fail to notice Arrow's smile and the way he looks at you.

You act like you're some kind of muscleman on Pismo Beach. Instead of pumping iron, you pump Iraqi kids, lifting them off the ground by twos, one off each bicep.

From their perches on the Humvee roofs, your gunners hear the giggles and it distracts them. It breaks their concentration, but that's okay because their brains have been on high alert for more than an hour and by now their eyes hurt after looking at the same doorways and storefronts, over and over. The gunners glance down at the other soldiers, the darting and dodging kids. The gunners grin, but then snap back to the mission at hand. They force themselves to turn their backs on their buddies talking and laughing with the kids. They scan another sector of fire, thinking all the while: *That Sergeant Morgan, man. He sure loves them kids.*

That's when the car, which had been prowling through an alley adjacent to the road, decides to make its move. For the past ten minutes, it has been rolling unseen through the neighborhood outside the military cordon, watching for a weakness in the line of Humvees, waiting for the right moment. The low-riding car is a lion, moving on whisper paws through the shadows of the grass, stalking with professional finesse, before it coils, then roars forward, the engine growling as the driver accelerates into the open for the kill.

Maybe one of the soldiers standing on the street looks up and knows exactly what is about to happen. Maybe he feels the weight of his mistake. Maybe he tries to scream, but the words stick in his throat. Maybe he raises his hands to push away the car—like he could do that, like he was a Marvel superhero. Or maybe those hands grab the two nearest children and pull them close in a protective embrace. One last effort to save the people of this country. Maybe that soldier prays, asks God to spare these two little girls.

Maybe that soldier is you.

The car bomb concusses the air, and we suffer hearing loss as sudden and deep as the time we had our annual exams at the troop medical clinic back at Fort Drum.

We remember being called in, as a group, to the hearing-test chamber—a small heavily carpeted room with padded walls and two rows of cubicle booths running its length. Large headphones hung on the pegboard wall in front of us as we sat down. We were told to place them on our heads and wait for further instructions.

The heavy earphones clamped tight as a vice against our skulls. When we put them on, we were underwater and the only thing we could hear was a ringing deep inside our skull that we thought at the time must have been a faint whine from the machinery of our brains.

A voice crackled—too loud—through the headphones, instructing us to pick up the handset, also hanging on the peg-board, and press the button whenever we heard a beep. The tones would come at various pitches and volumes. "Good luck and listen hard," the crackle voice said.

We sat on our stools, straining, closing our eyes—as if that would help—stopping all breath whistling in and out of our nostrils, all so we could hear the tones. Several of us pressed the call button, even though nothing was actually there. Some of us, the pranksters, went ahead and pressed the button in a regular pulse every three seconds, thinking one of those times they would land on the precise moment of a beep.

We froze in place. We stopped breathing. We went blank with silence.

That's how it was for us the moment Sergeant Morgan died: all sound gone in a suck.

Except, no—there was a faint whisper, a buzzing *tickle-ting* deep, deep, deep inside our heads. The whisper gradually came closer and grew louder and louder until it came out in a scream.

The explosion sucks all sound into a vacuum, turning this one acre of Baghdad into a silent film full of smoke and gore. In the silence, the suicide bomber's car incinerates with such force that later, when the fire hoses have doused and cooled the scene and the body parts have been marked with tiny flags and all the photos have been taken, the only thing that will remain for investigators to log into evidence is the engine block.

. Children fly into the air, cartwheeling, their bodies aflame. One boy will die with not a mark on him, but all of his clothes will be blown from his body and that very day, before the sun goes down, his sobbing father will place him in a coffin like that, naked and fetally curled. Seven or eight children—who can bear to look long enough to make an accurate count?—are flung against a wall in front of a house. Their bodies strike the bricks and collapse in a heap on the ground. If you didn't look too closely, you might think it was a pile of dirty clothes that need laundering. If you did look closer, however, you'd see a little girl abruptly sheared of both legs, her blackened face still cooking. A boy has died with both fists clenched. Inside those fists are Jolly Rancher candies. Another boy, not four feet away, has his hand raised toward his face, as if he is about to suck his thumb. There is a fist-size hole in his forehead, a neatly scooped hole that is so horribly, horribly out of place but yet so undeniably real in its seething red presence.

Back at the Humvees, someone is screaming. But no one can hear him because all sound has been sucked away and the only thing left is a high-pitched ringing that comes from within. This is a silent movie we're forced to watch: the smoke, the flames licking the engine block, the scattered children, the twelve dead (including one of the American soldiers), the eighteen wounded, the empty sandals, the pools of blood, the four half-shattered buildings, and the three Iraqi men rushing up with blankets to cover the dead.

When it happened, Arrow was turning to say something to Lieutenant Grimner. Thinking back on it now, he couldn't remember what it was. Maybe a complaint about next month's ten-on, one-off schedule; maybe it was a question about that night's dinner at the dining facility; maybe it was a joke about going on ghost patrols. Must not have been too important.

The explosion jolted everything from his head.

He heard, rather than saw—no, scratch that: *felt*, rather than heard—the car roaring across the open space. Arrow was seventy-five meters away from Sergeant Morgan, but the vibration of the engine rolled up his spine as if he himself had been standing in the path of the car.

He turned away from Lieutenant Grimner, with whatever he'd been about to say left unsaid on his tongue. For one nano-second, he was pissed at this thundercloud of noise interrupting his comment to the LT.

Arrow saw Sergeant Morgan grab those two little girls, pull them to him, and then there was a sudden puff of dust and metal, the flash already blossoming in orange petals that curled black in a blink.

He heard Lieutenant Grimner say, "Fu—"

Then everything went black and blank.

Until then, for the past two hours, the day had been hot, the mission boring. We'd been lulled half-asleep by the heat shimmering off the hoods of our Humvees. The wind pushed the dust through New Baghdad, same as always. Once the kids' demands for candy had dwindled, there had been nothing to hold our interest. Sure, we kept scanning the terrain, but once you've looked at the same doorway with four dozen sweeps of the eye, it gets pretty fucking old, okay? We felt the lullaby of the distant, bleating goats and the squeak of the gunners rotating in their sling seats, back and forth, back and forth, scan, scan, scan.

The day pulled on, dragging iron weights behind it.

Once, one of us announced he couldn't hold it any longer and relieved himself against the side of his Humvee. That held our interest for a while—the patter of piss hitting the tire—but then it was over and the soldier said, "Aaahhhh . . . the pause that refreshes." Someone else said something about it being better to be pissed *off* than pissed *on*, and we went back to what we'd been doing. We scanned our sectors of fire and the minutes trickled by too slow.

Sergeant Morgan circulated the line, checking for heat-stroke, squeezing Camelbaks to monitor water levels, commiserating with the occasional: "Yeah, this sucks balls all right."

One or two of us—including Sergeant Morgan himself—hadn't been able to resist playing grab ass with the kids who still hung around the perimeter. Cross-cultural international relations, that's what Sergeant Morgan called it—and he was the worst offender of us all, the way he got into it with the kids. Rafe pretended he was a carnival sideshow strongman by lifting two thin Iraqi girls off the ground, one on each side of him. The girls, kind of cute even with their rat's-nest hair and snot-crusted noses, giggled as they held on to Sergeant Morgan's biceps and rose two feet off the ground when he curled his arms upward. They dangled like bracelets off this funny American.

We laughed along with the girls.

But Rafe was always like that, flexing his strength for all to see. He must have thought it was some funny shit to be doing curls with those girls. He probably would have liked how that sounded: girl curls.

He was cool, that Rafe. Oh, he came off badass, tough as a cement wall, but deep down he was a give-the-shirt-off-his-back kind of guy. He was strong and he took that strength seriously, like it was his personal mission to protect the weaker ones around him. This is how he was with all of us, not just those Iraqi girls. He thought of the other person first, himself last.

That's why nobody was surprised when we later pieced it together, what we'd seen out of the corner of our eyes. It was typical of Rafe to react like he did, going into protector mode by instinct. When he realized the car was coming right at him, Sergeant Morgan pulled those girls tight against his chest, wrapping himself around them as best he could. He must have known it was a useless gesture, that he was flesh and not iron, but what else can you do in that split-second of reflex? You're gonna obey the synaptic impulse of your nerves and the reflexive pull of your muscles, right? You're gonna grab those girls and hold on tight. You're gonna duck your head, let the top of your helmet take the brunt of whatever's coming your way. You're gonna tuck yourself over those two little heads, the three of you breathing together in that tight space for the smallest of moments. You might even manage to gasp "hold on" to these girls who have no idea what the words are but must sense what they mean.

Hold on, here we go. Like the three of them had reached the crest of a rollercoaster and were hovering on the plunge.

From where he stood, seventy-five meters away, Specialist Dmitri Arogapoulos didn't actually *see* the incinerating evaporation of Sergeant Raphael Morgan, but he *felt* it. Oh fuck yeah, he felt it all the way to the marrow. As Arrow fell to the ground, pushed there by the concussion and cradled in the vacuum of silence, he thought it was just him. Maybe he was having a stroke or a blackout or something. For that sliver of time, he was embarrassed and thought how the rest of us would be sure to give him a rash of shit for passing out like a pussy.

Then, over his head, he saw the cloud of boiling blooming smoke, and he thought maybe it *wasn't* just him. Maybe it was all of us. Maybe we were all dead.

But when the body parts and bits of flesh started raining on Arrow, he knew for certain it wasn't him. It wasn't any of us. It took him a moment to slide back to the realization he was still alive, and then another moment to realize this was Sergeant Morgan falling from the sky.

51
ECP

We are equal parts brilliant and dumb. This becomes apparent when we approach the Entry Control Point to FOB Saro. We had a plan, but then that plan went all to shit and we had to improvise, like a jazz saxophonist who loses his place halfway through "Birdland." Now we're flinging notes all over the place, hoping they'll stick.

We've been gliding along Route Irish with the rest of the traffic, zipping down the main thoroughfare with the Opels, the Saabs, the semis, the occasional coalition forces Humvee, with nobody giving us a second look. Yeah, we're just a bunch of American soldiers rattling along in a hajji van, what of it? We're dumb, we're brilliant, and we're in a hurry to finish the mission.

And then we see the concrete turret off to our left.

Arrow goes, "There it is! There it is!" like he was on a whale-watching cruise in Alaska.

"I see it," Fish says.

"Go left! Go left!"

"I got it, Arrow."

Fish moves to the left-turn lane, waits for a break in traffic, then swings us down a road toward the T-walls, the guard shack, the barrier arm the guards raise and lower like a drawbridge.

ECPs are checkpoints, choke points, pinch points, funnels, X-ray machines, sieves, sorters, and separators. ECPs separate us from them, America from Baghdad, the wheat from the chaff. ECPs are the first and last line of defense. Nothing bad gets through, nothing suspicious will penetrate.

Right now, in our dust-caked van with Arabic lettering on the side and a big metal daisy sticking up from the roof, we are all kinds of suspicious. We're a beetle with a new shell and, for the moment, in our eagerness to get onto Saro, we've forgotten what our makeshift carapace looks like from the outside.

We're barreling forward in the van, racing the clock because O is bleeding out on the floor in the back and beside him, a baby is trying to come into the world. We think only of Olijandro, and maybe a little of the pregnant woman, too, as Fish steers toward the concrete barriers.

When we see the guard step out of the ECP and raise his M4, that's when it hits us, our stupid stupidity, and Arrow yells, "Wait! Stop!"

52

FOB Saro

"Wait! Stop!"

Fish jams his foot on the brake and the van rocks to a halt two hundred yards from the concrete barrier. Rising dust blurs everything for a moment. Words blare at us from a loudspeaker mounted at the top of the guard shack but we can't make them out because there's an ocean roar of blood in our ears.

We feel the burn of our mistake.

The barrel of the guard's M4 doesn't waver. He stares at us, tightens his eyes to a squint, puts his cheek to the stock of the rifle.

"No, no, no!" Arrow screams through the dirty windshield.

"Back up! Back up!" Drew yells, but Fish has already thrown the van in reverse and is moving away from the Entry Control Point.

More tinny words come at us in a blizzard of static.

Fish stops after twenty-five yards and Arrow opens his door.

"Careful, man," Drew says.

Arrow looks back at him. "No shit." He looks at Fish. "Follow me in the van. But slow and steady." He raises his arms, steps in front of the van, and walks forward. He's left his rifle in the van. It leans against his empty seat.

Fish rolls forward, gravel crackling under the van's tires.

The speaker continues to blare at us, louder now and higher pitched. Another rifle pokes out of the slit in the turret.

Arrow walks forward with his hands in the air.

The loudspeaker gives two shouts and Arrow yells something back, but in the next instant two shots ring out. Arrow dives to the left as asphalt chips in a puff of dust ten feet in front of him. Fish brakes 150 yards out from the barrier.

Arrow screams, spread-eagled on the pavement.

The next rounds, when they come, will puncture the van's grille. After that, according to the rules of engagement, we know we can expect the bullets to shatter the windshield and bore straight into our heads, if these guys are good shots—and, from what we can see, they are.

Our hearts thump. Our scalps burn with prickles. Our mouths go slack.

Even the woman has fallen silent. She knows what's going on. Maybe she's had her car fired on once or twice when she was out grocery shopping.

The two gate guards come at us, walking with rifles against their cheeks, slow and steady.

Cheever moves to open the side door.

"Don't!" Drew yells. "That could make it worse."

Cheever has the door slid halfway back before he stops.

"But—but—" he sputters. "Can't they see we're on the same team? Our uniforms—"

"Iraqis can steal a set of DCUs same as anyone else," Park says.

"We need to go help Arrow." Now Cheever has a boot out the door.

"Cheeve!" Fish yells. "Stop! Please."

It's the "please" that does it. Fish isn't known for his *pleases* and *thank yous*.

Cheever gets back in the van.

"No sudden moves," Fish says. "All nice and calm now, okay?" He's staring out the window, talking to himself as much as he is to the rest of us.

We hunker down below dashboard level. Arrow, Mr. Big Balls himself, can take it from here. We hope.

O, nestled between the dry husks of what were once tulips and roses, breathes shallow. His eyes are glazed and his skin is paper white.

"O," we say. "O."

O, at ease in his bed of flowers, smells the ghost of a bouquet he once gave his ex-wife. No, wife—his *wife*. Their fourth anniversary. Roses, dyed lavender because that was her favorite color at the time. They'd been having a bad week because she thought he'd forgotten their anniversary. Melinda was all stony silences and averted eyes, acting like he hadn't been picking up any of the hints she'd dropped, breadcrumbs strewn in the path before him. He saw the back of her head a lot that week. What did she know? He heard everything. He listened and absorbed, dammit.

That's why, when he showed up at her workplace, standing at the front desk of the fitness club with a fistful of lavender roses and, in his pocket, the earrings she'd pointed out in the glass case at Costco a month earlier, O had a big, goofy grin on his face. He couldn't *wait* to see her expression when she came through the doors from the towel room. He would be redeemed, dammit, re-fucking-deemed.

God, these roses smell good, he thinks now in the back of the van. He closes his eyes and sinks back into the flowers. The petals crackle and crumble behind his head.

And then he is running across that field again and he is reaching the other side and he is taking Melinda in his arms.

"O!" we cry. We put our hands on him, as if to pull him back, but it's no use.

He's gone.

We sit back, stunned. This can't be happening. No. No no *no*. This isn't real, is it?

The woman breaks our silence with a sharp cry. She bucks her hips, arches her back.

Cheever feels something odd and fluffy well up inside him. He scoots across the van to be by her side. He takes her hand and lets her grip him hard as she can. He doesn't care. In fact, he hopes she'll break his fingers so he can feel her pain.

Outside, on the pavement, Arrow is totally focused on the dark mouths of the rifle barrels coming toward him.

"Guys," he calls out. He coughs against a tickle of dust in his throat. All he can think to do is call out his name, rank, and unit. Just like in a goddamn movie. He repeats his name over and over until the rifles halt their advance and one of them goes to sling arms while the other barrel keeps pointing at Arrow's head.

A pair of boots approaches, then stops ten feet away.

Arrow tries to lift his head, but his helmet stops him from going very far. "Friendly," he coughs. "We're friendlies."

A voice, high and thin with a Tennessee twang, says from far above, "Well, Jesus Harvey Christ! We thought you was al-Qaeda or something. Welcome to FOB Saro, you lucky son of a bitch."

53

Zero to Hero

Arrow is inside the Entry Control Point's shack, talking to one of the guards. There are a lot of hand gestures on Arrow's part.

The other ECP guard stands between the van and the small shack. Like he's gonna stop the van from rolling through into the base.

This gate, the one we've stumbled on, is in a remote corner of FOB Saro. There is no one else around except us, the two guards, and a plastic bag skipping across the road to the barrier fence, which it hugs like a lover.

Arrow is still talking. It doesn't look like he's getting anywhere.

From inside the van, Fish goes, "Fuck this." He pulls the keys from the ignition, grabs his rifle, and gets out.

"Where you going, Fish?"

"Just gonna go have a talk with this guy, Drew."

"Arrow said to—"

"Chill, Drew, chill. Doesn't look like we're going anywhere soon." Fish slams the door shut and walks toward the ECP.

Cheever grumbles, "So I can't get out, but *he* can?"

Drew goes, "Not like we could stop him. Fish being Fish."

The guard at the barrier tightens the grip on his rifle as Fish walks up. He's a short guy shaped like a bulldog. The way he wears his sunglasses, he obviously thinks he's Hollywood. A walkie-talkie is clipped to the shoulder of his flak vest like a badge he wants to make sure you see.

"Hold it right there," he says in a high, guitar-string voice.

"Relax, brother. We're the good guys here. See?" Fish points to the US flag embroidered on his shoulder.

"I've been told to keep the rest of you in the van."

"I just want to ask you something."

Fish is right up on him now, but the guard doesn't raise his weapon, keeps it low and easy at belt level. That's his first mistake.

His second mistake is allowing Fish to keep his own M4 slung over his shoulder. We don't know for sure, but this might be the dumbest soldier in the United States Army. If he really thinks we're a threat, he would have taken Fish's rifle right away.

Third mistake: Fish gets to ask his question.

"You got a cigarette I can borrow? I mean *have*?"

The guard wavers. "Yeah, sure," he says, taking one hand off his rifle to dig in his cargo pocket. He hands Fish a crumpled pack. Fourth mistake. "Keep it. There's only two left anyway."

"Thanks, man." Fish pretends to look for something, pats his pockets. "You got a light, too?"

The guard hands him a lighter.

"Thanks." Fish tries to light his cigarette, but there is wind—the same breeze that pushed the bag into the fence.

Fish goes, "You think we could step around the back of the guard shack so we're out of the wind?"

The guard looks at the van.

Fish goes, "Don't worry about them. They aren't going anywhere. I've got the keys." He pulls the key ring out of his pocket and jangles it in the guard's face.

The guard sighs. "Okay, fine."

They walk behind the turret. Fish lights his cigarette, then leans back against the barrier arm.

Fish goes, "Shit, what a day." He holds the smoke in his lungs as long as he can, then lets it drift from his lips like slow-creeping fog.

"What've you guys been doing out there?"

"Just walking."

Arrow comes out of the guard shack alone. He starts toward the van, then stops when he sees Fish out back with the other guard. "Fish?"

Fish waves to him. "Hey, Arrow."

"What's up?"

"Nothing much. Just having a smoke and a chat. I'll be right over."

Arrow goes, "Make it snappy," then gets in the van.

"That your squad leader?" the guard asks.

"He likes to think he is."

"What's with the van, anyway?"

Fish looks at the flower-topped cargo van. He sees Arrow turn in the front seat, then lunge toward the back as he gets the news about O. A muffled cry of grief rises from the van. All falls silent for a few seconds, then a female voice begins her ascendency along a scale of pain once more, huffing a series of notes that go "Oo-ooo-oooo!"

Fish turns back to the gate guard, picking a fleck of tobacco off his tongue. "Like I said, we were walking. And then we got tired so we kind of hijacked the van."

"Hijacked it? Shit."

"It's a long story. We'll sit down over a couple of beers one day and I'll tell you the whole thing."

"Who're you guys with, anyway? Third Herd?"

"Tenth Mountain."

"Tenth Mountain? I thought they were up at Taji."

"They are. We are."

"So what're you doing here in the city?"

"We're just out for a walk. Like I said."

Now the guard is looking like he wishes he didn't give Fish those cigarettes. He grips his rifle and holds it higher.

"I think you need to go finish your smoke in the van."

"I'd rather stay right here and finish it. Then I'll go back to the van."

"No, you need to—"

The walkie on the gate guard's shoulder crackles. He half turns from Fish and speaks into it, listens, and speaks again, signing off, then turns back to Fish. "You're to wait here."

Fish laughs. "First you tell me I need to get in the van and now you say I need to stay put. Which is it, Einstein?"

"I mean you all need to wait here. At the ECP."

Fish pulls in another lung of smoke, holds it, then releases it, this time in a sharp, hard puff. "Okay, look. There's something else I need to tell you. We're kind of in a hurry. We've got an appointment we need to get to. It's somewhere else here

242

on the FOB, so we can't afford to sit around and wait here all afternoon."

"Well, looks like it *will* have to wait."

"It can't wait."

"Sorry, higher says to keep you here for now."

"Higher, huh?"

"Yeah. You know, the head shed. My higher."

"Look, I'm asking you to let us do one little thing and then we'll be done."

"Higher says—"

"Just one small thing," Fish insists. "It'll take twenty minutes, max. We go do this one thing, and we'll come right back here. Then we're all yours. Higher can do whatever they're gonna do to us."

"Sorry," the guard says. "I've been told to keep you here."

"I understand. That's probably what I'd do, too, I was in your shoes. Unless I had a better option."

"Buddy, there are no other options. Higher says keep you, I keep you."

Fish nods. In the time since we first arrived, there's been no other traffic, no other vehicles approaching the ECP. What kind of sleepy, backwater FOB is this place anyway? Fish looks around. The nearest building is a half mile away and it looks deserted. The road leading from the guard shack is cracked, weeds poking out of the macadam. The guard shack is small, big enough for two of them, maybe one chair. No other equipment—no computers or cameras, just a walkie and their weapons. There's not even a shitter nearby. These guys must be a pair of grade-A fucktards to draw the short straw for this duty.

Fish smiles at the guard. "Let me ask you something."

"Okay."

"Do you want to be a hero or a zero?"

"What?"

"Do you want to be a hero or do you want to be a zero?"

The guard chuffs in dismissal. "I don't like my options."

"Why not?"

"Zeros are . . . well, zeros. And heroes usually end up getting killed."

"What if I said you could be a hero and stay alive? A twofer deal."

The guard shakes his head. "I don't even know why we're having this conversation. You all need to sit tight, shut up, and wait until we get further instructions from higher."

The wind kicks up again, makes the weeds in the road shiver.

Fish goes, "What's your name, private?"

"Abernathy. Obviously." The guard points to his name tape.

"I meant your first name."

"David. Why?"

"I'll say again: Do you want to be a hero or a zero, David?"

"This again, huh?" Abernathy sighs. "Okay, I'll play along. A hero. Why?"

"Not *why*. *How*."

"Okay, how?"

"You get on the horn and tell them you're bringing us in to higher yourself."

"When?"

"Right now."

"You're out of your mind, dude. I can't leave the ECP. Duncan gets left alone, he'll freak out. Besides, I'd get an Article Fifteen for abandoning my post."

"What time's shift change?"

"Any minute now."

"Okay, we wait for any minute to arrive, then you take us."

"You're nuts."

"No, I'm desperate. Like I said, we've got someplace to be. What time's it, anyway?"

"Nearly sixteen hundred."

"Shit," Fish says.

"You miss your appointment?"

"Most of it. But there might still be something left. We just need to get there."

Abernathy looks back at the guard shack. Fish gives him a minute to think without putting on any more pressure.

The guard shakes his head. "I don't know about any of this."

"What don't you know? You take us to higher headquarters, easy peasy. We're going there anyway. Only difference is, you take us, and you take us right now."

"This all sounds pretty hinky."

"Nothing hinky about it, Abernathy. It's all on the up-and-up."

"Besides, why should I take you? Higher is sending some cops down here to pick you up."

Fish goes all electric. "They're *what?*"

"You heard me. MPs are on their way right now."

"Why didn't you tell me this before?"

Abernathy grins. "It never came up in conversation."

"Well, shit, Abernathy. This changes everything."

Fish raises his M4, pulls back the charging handle, then lays the muzzle against the side of Abernathy's head, gentle as a kiss. The grin falls off the kid's face, goes splat in the dirt at their feet.

"Whoa! Whoa whoa whoa!"

"You should have told me about the MPs."

"Fucking A, man! Fucking A! This is some UCMJ shit right here. That's what this is!"

"Keep it down, Abernathy." Fish looks over at the guard shack. The other guy hasn't even poked his head out. He must be either scared, lazy, or deaf. One thing's for sure—he's just edged out Abernathy for the title of Worst Soldier in the World.

Fish reaches over and takes the rifle from the guard's hands. Never mind. Abernathy has the crown back now.

"Jesus Harvey Christ! I thought you said this was gonna be on the up-and-up."

"Not anymore."

Arrow gets out of the van. His face is pinched. He's still dealing with O, but now *this* is happening—everything sliding out of control again. He spreads his hands: *What the fuck?*

Fish waves back: *We're cool.*

"This is so wrong," Abernathy whimpers.

"You left me no choice."

"Bullshit. Jesus God, man, you can't wait to see the inside of Leavenworth, can you?"

"To be honest, I don't care right now." He taps Abernathy's helmet with the tip of the barrel. "It's been a long day. And you're wasting my time trying to decide whether you should shit your pants right now or hold it for later."

Arrow starts toward them. Fish holds up a hand to stop him. He's got this, no cause for alarm, boys and girls. Arrow shakes his head, but gets back in the van.

We wait and watch for the next move.

Fish goes, "Okay, Abernathy. Here comes your big moment."

"You are in such deep shit, man."

"I want you to go over and poke your head in the guard shack—just your head—and tell what's-his-name—"

"Duncan."

"And tell Duncan you just got a call on your walkie from higher saying the MPs got diverted and now they're authorizing you to bring us in. And that you cleared it with your sergeant of the guard—what's his name?"

"Staff Sergeant Molina."

"That you cleared it with Sergeant Molina and he, Duncan, is supposed to sit tight until shift change, which is any minute now, and you'll meet him later at the chow hall and tell him all about it. Then you walk around our van, nice and easy, and get behind the wheel."

"Duncan'll never buy it."

"So you *make* him buy it." Fish gives a barrel tap on Abernathy's helmet at each word.

Abernathy, calmer now, says, "You're bluffing. You won't shoot me."

Fish raises the rifle to his shoulder. A look comes into his eyes. "Take a guess at how many people I've killed. Not counting today. It's no big deal for me to do it one more time. Go ahead. See if I'm bluffing."

Fish thinks of Charles Yardley, bleeding from his eighteen wounds.

Abernathy sees the look in Fish's eyes. His mouth is too dry for him to speak, so he just nods.

"We're wasting time. Make up your mind. Is it yes or no? Do I air-condition your head or do you go along to get along as my sergeant used to say?"

Abernathy takes two and a half seconds to decide. Then he goes along to get along.

He pokes his head—just his head—in the guard shack and says something in a low voice to Duncan. It's down low enough so Fish can't hear and that worries him, so he slips the barrel tip underneath the back lip of Abernathy's helmet.

And so the kid sells it. He sells it good to Duncan because all Fish hears is an "okay, whatever, dude" from the other guard. It's said in the kind of end-of-shift-and-I-don't-give-a-shit voice.

Abernathy pulls his head back out and nods at Fish. He goes nice and easy to the driver's side.

"This is fucked up."

"No commentary, Abernathy. We've had a long day and we're not in the mood."

Abernathy gets in. Fish gets in. Abernathy looks back at the rest of us. We have our weapons pointed at him.

Abernathy goes, "They better have one big shiny medal waiting for me at headquarters."

"Oh, I never said you'd be a hero to higher, Abernathy."

"Who then?"

"Us." Fish smiles. "You're our hero."

The guard looks over his shoulder again. We nod back at him.

Abernathy catches sight of the woman. "Whoa whoa whoa!"

"Take it easy," Arrow says.

"Who the fuck is she?"

"She's with us."

"Yeah, but look at her. Just look at her."

The woman's legs are spread. Things are about to get serious. Cheever is wiping her forehead and Lamaze breathing with her.

Fish says, "Don't worry about her, Abernathy. We've got this under control."

"Yeah, but what's her story?"

"Never mind about her," Arrow says.

Fish goes, "Yeah, just drive. Unless *you* want to be the story. You wanna be a headline in tomorrow's paper, Abernathy?"

"Jesus Harvey Christ!" Now he's seen O's body and we want to butt-stroke him because he's acting irreverent in the presence of the dead, but we need Abernathy to get us through Saro, so we let it pass—for now. There will be time enough for butt-strokes later.

Then Arrow says, "Just get us to the church on time."

Abernathy frowns. "The church? What church?"

"Oh yeah," Fish says. "I guess I forgot to mention we have one little stop along the way."

54

Memorial

The chapel is straight off a Vermont postcard. But instead of blazing orange maples and red oaks, the church lies between a withered palm tree and an empty field pocked with craters from incoming mortars.

Somebody wanted this chapel to scream: "Holy!" and "America!"

It was built quickly, as if KBR contractors ordered it out of a Sears catalog, then assembled it from a kit here in Baghdad. Insert tab A into slot B, then glue the steeple in place, hallelujah and amen.

There's no one around, no cars parked outside the chapel.

We check our watches. 1606. Sixty-six minutes late.

Dammit.

We're deflated but not defeated. We made it, and that was the point. Success is reaching the end of the game with a high score and all your lives, right?

Well, almost.

We look at O. We can't talk about him. Not now. Maybe later.

Arrow goes, "Well, we're here."

Drew goes, "Gee, that hardly took any time at all."

We stare at the chapel as we pull into the parking lot. It's smaller than we'd imagined it would be. Just enough room for a platoon of grieving soldiers.

We tell Abernathy to pull up next to the front door. He hasn't said much the whole ride. We get the feeling he knows there's something serious going on. He'll shut up now and let us do our thing.

We get out of the van. Two of us—Arrow and Park—reach back inside and lift O out. We're the gentlest of pallbearers.

We leave the woman inside. We wish her all the best, but she was never part of the deal.

Cheever is still Lamaze breathing with her and we hate to pull him away, but we have to finish this together.

When he sees we've arrived at the chapel, Cheever nods and gets out of the van.

Arrow bends at the knees and pulls O across his shoulders. He'll be the one to carry him these final steps.

From her bed of flowers inside the van, the woman pants and groans. Cheever goes back for one last look. The woman's hair has come loose and a thick strand is sweat-plastered across her forehead like a comma. She stares at Cheever and he thinks he knows what she's trying to say.

"You're welcome," he whispers. He turns to Abernathy. "Keep your eye on her."

"Okay. But you're coming right back, right?"

We ignore him and turn toward the finish line.

Park carries Arrow's rifle. Drew and Fish follow slowly. Cheever is still sympathy breathing with the woman. He's so far out of himself at this point, he forgets to limp on his blisters.

Arrow, bent beneath the weight of O, stops and turns to us. He goes, "Ready?"

We go, "Ready."

We open the door. We enter the chapel.

Hoover, the chaplain's assistant, is the only one inside. Our company commander, our first sergeant, our fellow soldiers in mourning, they all left a long time ago. They're already putting Sergeant Morgan behind them.

Hoover is at the front of the empty sanctuary, folding cloths and packing them into boxes. At the sound of our boots, he looks up.

He goes, "Holy mother of fuck," soft as a prayer.

There is nothing left of Sergeant Morgan's memorial. Correction: there is one thing left—his boots. Correction: his boot—singular. The right one. It's at the front of the sanctuary, on display at the center of a three-tiered pedestal that once held a rifle, two boots, and a photo of Rafe smiling at the camera. Now there is just a single empty boot. Hoover has packed everything else away.

We walk up the center aisle single file, Arrow and O in the lead, then Park, then Drew, then Fish, then Cheever bringing up the rear. A sad parade of the footsore and heavyhearted.

We advance and Hoover drops the cloths he'd been holding. He stammers: "You, you guys weren't supposed to . . . Captain Bangor told us you were . . . You're AWOL, and you . . ."

We are deaf to Hoover. He could be explaining the Periodic Table of Elements for all we care. We hear nothing but our boot steps and the beat of our hearts.

Arrow arrives at the front of the sanctuary first. He bends, shrugs O off his shoulders, then places him in a pew. He makes sure O stays upright, his hands in his lap, head tilted so he can see everything. Arrow has brought us this far, he'll make sure everyone is there at the end. Dead or alive.

With a wrench of our hearts, we realize we'll be doing this all over again in a few days for O.

We can't think about that right now. It's beyond what we can bear on this day.

Hoover clears his throat. "If you're here for Sergeant Morgan's service, you know you're too late."

At his name, we fall silent.

Arrow goes, "Let's do this, boys."

He thinks: *Shit, I sound just like him.*

Arrow smiles. Then he remembers that last flicker he saw of Rafe from the corner of his eye—the way he bent and hugged those two little girls close to his chest. Arrow wishes he could be those girls. He would hold Rafe and never let go.

Arrow elbows Hoover aside, then takes a knee. We surround him in a half circle and each take a knee as well.

We stare at the lone boot on the pedestal at the altar. It is clean and the laces are neatly tucked inside.

We're silent with our thoughts about Sergeant Morgan.

Behind us, beyond the open chapel doors, we hear a siren. We turn our heads. We see Abernathy get out of the driver's seat and run around to the back of the van. Then we realize that's no siren. It's the woman. The contractions are coming harder and harder now. She screams the baby into the world.

We turn back and look at Sergeant Morgan's boot.

We each reach out a hand to touch this last part of Rafe that remains. Without warning, our breath bucks and pitches in our lungs and we release what has been in there all this time. We've held it for four days. That's long enough.

We're all weeping now. Not loud, but not silently, either. We don't care who sees our tears, our crumpled faces—not Hoover, not the absent Captain Bangor, not Rafe's ghost, not even if every pew in the church was filled with our girlfriends, wives, sons and daughters, and George Bush himself.

As we say our last good-bye, we cry, we cry, we cry.

Acknowledgments

On this novel's long walk to publication, many people offered encouragement and to these I owe immeasurable thanks:

My agent, Nat Sobel, who gave early pages of *Brave Deeds* a much-needed morale boost during lunch at the legendary Pete's Tavern on East 18th St. in 2014. As the spirit of O. Henry (a Pete's Tavern regular) watched over us, Nat said he saw great possibilities for what was then, in my mind, a mess of a manuscript. Among other things, Nat suggested I read a little-remembered novel first published in 1944 . . .

A Walk in the Sun by Harry N. Brown proved, as all good war literature should, that courage is no walk in the park. An even larger debt of gratitude goes to Richard Bausch and his slim, masterful novel *Peace* (2008), which was always the brightest lamppost guiding *Brave Deeds* along its path.

My Book Pregnant posse at Facebook, who held my hand and coached me through birthing pains as I carried this book baby to term long past its due date.

Chris McCann, editor of *The Arctic Warrior* (the newspaper for US Army Alaska soldiers and families), who came to the Great Harvest Bread Company in Anchorage, Alaska, in 2013 for the very first public reading of *Brave Deeds* (an early draft of the first chapter) and unwittingly gave me the gift of christening FOB Saro.

Rosalie Kearns for assistance with the Spanish language passages.

My fellow warriors of the pen Benjamin Busch, Matt Gallagher, and Phil Klay, who were there with advice when I needed it the most.

My brilliant copy editor, Paula Cooper Hughes, who asked all the right questions, stitched up plot holes, and helped me bring fuzzy characters into sharper focus.

My editor Peter Blackstock and the entire Grove Atlantic team: bright stars in the literary galaxy, each and every one of them. Peter—my 3-W friend (wit, wisdom, and warmth)—brought this book across the finish line, cheering me every step of the way. He is my compass, my map, my headlights on a dark road.

And last, but far from least, my beloved Jean. She may not be my first reader, but she is always the most important one.